The Protector

And the legend of the swans

By JenniferM.Beagon

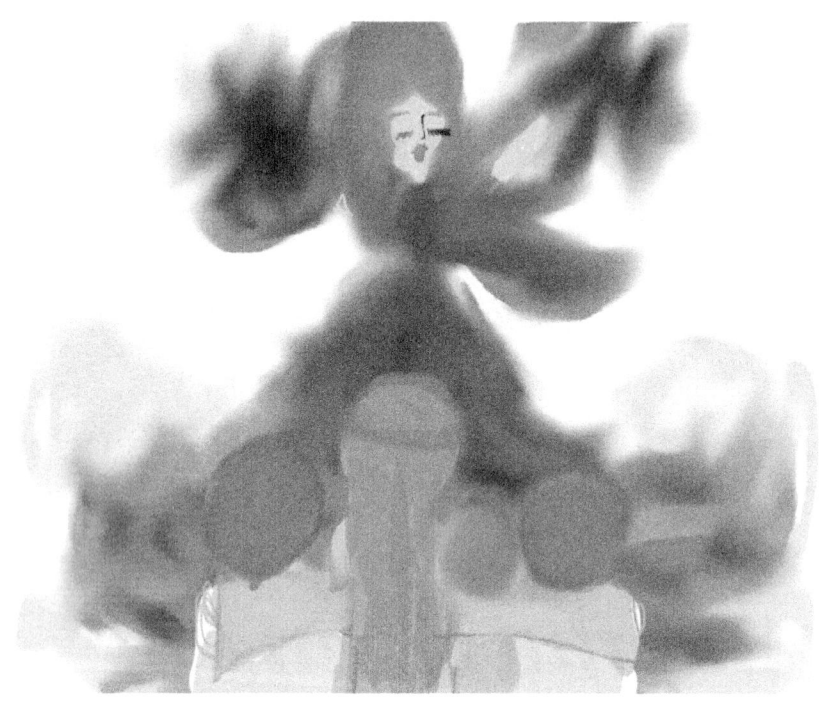

Prologue

Fidelma was lying on her bed in her room. Outside the rain battered against the window and the wind howled like a pained animal, she was thinking that it always seemed to rain when there was a funeral but then she thought if that was the case it would be constantly raining, well she lived in Ireland, so who knows, maybe that was the case.

The funeral she had been to that day was her Grandmothers and the sadness that Fidelma felt was overwhelming, right now the sound of the wild night outside her window felt like a reflection of her soul, the heavy rain, the tears that just kept coming and the wind, the feeling of pain and emptiness inside her. Granny Fidelma always seemed younger than her years, always full of fun and telling stories, hard to believe then that she was 96 when she died just 3 days ago, but Fidelma was feeling like she had been very hard done by, she loved her Granny more than anything and had been extremely close to her. The youngest of 12 grandchildren Fidelma had been called after her Granny and had always felt a strong connection to her.

She could hear the rumble of voices downstairs as people reminisced about her Granny, and she knew it was only a matter of time before the talking turned to singing, she also knew that this was what Irish people did and it was their respectful way of mourning, but still Fidelma did not want to be part of it, all she wanted to do was cry and wallow in her grief.

Chapter 1:

Fidelma was rushing around her bedroom looking for her phone when she heard her Mother call up to her "Fidelma? Are you gonna come with me?"

"*Fidelma?*"

"Yes Mam, I hear ye" Fidelma sat on her bed trying to decide what she wanted to do, her Mother and her Aunties were all meeting at Grannys house this morning to sort through her things, knowing Granny, it would be a long day, or two! Fidelma pulled on her Ugg boots, a treasured present from her big brother Sean from his year in Australia, and ran downstairs, "ok Mam I'm coming!"

The drive over to Granny Fidlemas house was quiet apart from the familiar voice of Joe Duffy coming from the radio; Mother and daughter were both lost in their own thoughts as Mrs. Doyle navigated her way through the morning traffic, thankful the secondary schools had started their summer holidays so the roads were not too busy.

Granny Fidelmas house was eerily quiet; it seemed like the land where time stood still were it not for the loud tick tock of the big Grandfather clock in the hallway. The house still had that familiar smell of Granny, a strong soapy smell mixed with that smell of old stuff. Everything looked the same; the same as it always had except Granny was not there, filling the house with her loveliness. Hanging on an old coat stand in the hallway was Grannys old coat, a powder blue mac that she had had for years, Fidelma touched the sleeve before leaning into it with her nose and inhaling the scent that still lingered there, she then quickly wiped at her eyes with the back of her hand and opened the door in front of her that led into the living area of the old house. This all felt so weird to Fidelma, it had been 3 weeks now since

Granny passed away and she still could not get her head around it, she just missed her so much. From the time Fidelma was a toddler she would sit on her Grannys knee listening to the most fascinating stories where Granny would paint Ireland as a magical mythical place that Fidelma longed to visit, she often wondered how her Granny remembered them all without reading from a book, the adventures were endless. Fidelma suddenly thought how wonderful it would be to just jump into one of those mythical stories now and forget about the empty hole she was feeling.

Fidelmas Mother was busy greeting her sisters who were sat at the old kitchen table, not surprisingly they had decided to start off with a cup of tea, Granny would be proud. Fidelma smiled and said hello to her aunties as she looked around the room, there were some boxes on the floor with clear labels on them in Grannys handwriting, she had known her end was near and just like always, she prided herself on being organised. Fidelma passed on the offer of tea and opted instead to take a ramble upstairs in the old house. There were three bedrooms upstairs, two of which had remained empty for many years apart from when the grandchildren stayed over which to be fair was quiet often, especially Fidelma, she stayed over most weekends, she loved getting up early on a Sunday morning and going to mass with Granny before spending a few blissful hours in the fairy garden, well, it was Grannys back garden but for as far back as she remembered that was what Granny had called it and Fidelma always felt that it was just the sort of garden where fairies would be happy. Unlike the front garden which was small, tidy and well groomed, the back garden was a bit on the wild side, a large old oak tree stood at the very back domineering the big garden which was full of wild flowers and over grown bushes, there were bird houses and feeders scattered throughout and little stone steps that seemed to lead to nowhere but to a child this was an enchanted place to play in and feed their imagination.

The door to Grannys bedroom was open and for a moment Fidelma just stood at the entrance looking in. Grannys big old bed, dark shiny wood with a bright and airy floral bedspread and a colourful crochet blanket at the end which Granny had made herself when she was just a girl, plenty of nights Fidelma had climbed in and snuggled up

with Granny in this bed. She went in
and sat on the end of the bed, the
matteress was high and springy.
Fidelma ran her hand along the
colourful blanket; it was old but
still soft beneath her touch. The big
dark wardrobe and dresser looked like
they were a hundred years old, but
then again, she supposed they could
well have been. Fidelma looked over at
the dresser, it was filled with little
knick knacks, mostly little statuettes
of fairies that Granny had collected
over the years, she walked over to
look at them as she had done so many
times before, at the back she noticed
a gap, Fidelma frowned, that was where

Grannys treasure chest used to be, she wondered briefly where it went to but did not linger on it, it had always been locked anyway.

Half an hour had passed before Fidelma decided to rejoin the others downstairs, when she walked into the kitchen her Mother and Aunties were laughing but at the same time wiping their noses and eyes, she sometimes forgot that it must be very hard for them too; after all they had just lost their Mammy.

"Ok Fidelma" said Auntie Mary "This one is for you" She handed Fidelma the missing treasure chest from Grannys dresser, Fidelma ran her hand along the fine detailing on it, something else she had done manys a time before. It looked like a real pirates treasure chest and as a child Fidelma had always believed it to be, sure Granny often told her about how she was given it as a present from a mermaid she once met while on holidays as a young girl in County Kerry, but of course Fidelma was 15 now, almost 16 in fact so she knew that mermaids and indeed fairies were not real and that these things could be picked up in plenty of shops. Still, she smiled at the memory of the story her Granny had told her and she felt her eyes fill up again.

It was late in the evening when Fidelma got back home with her Mother, they were exhausted but both smiling, it had been a lovely day, each sharing old memories of Granny. Later in the day a couple of Fidelmas older cousins had come by too, they had all drank plenty of tea and talked till the cows came home. She was sure Granny was smiling down on them all too, enjoying the reminiscing.

Once home, Fidelma went straight to her room to find a suitable place for her treasure chest, she sat with it on her lap for a few minutes feeling strangely sad, she was very happy to have the chest, she had always admired it, but deep down she had been hoping to get Grannys beloved charm bracelet. Fidelma hated even thinking this way as she knew it seemed selfish but she could not help how she felt. Granny had told her that she had gotten the charm bracelet from *her* Granny when she was very young, it only had one charm on it then but was now full of beautiful little charms, bought by family members over the years. Fidelma had always loved it; she would delicately finger the tiny charms as she sat with Granny. There were a few different charms on the bracelet; fairies and unicorns being the main theme, Fidelma wondered who got the bracelet; she had not heard them talk about it at Grannys house so she did not mention it for the fear of sounding ungrateful for the chest, still though, she could not help but wonder.

Chapter 2:

3 weeks later:

Fidelma was sitting in the living room flicking through the latest catalogue her Mother had got, she loved the clothes in it, some very cool outfits but not too expensive, she was thinking she might ask if she could order something nice from it for her birthday, she was going to be sixteen in two weeks and would love something a bit more grown up for going for the family dinner that was planned. Fidelma was really looking forward to it; cinema and bowling with 5 of her friends during the day then out with the family for dinner that evening. The doorbell interrupted her daydreaming and she heard her Mother chat to Aaron at the front door before sending him into Fidelma, she smiled, Aaron was her trusty old friend, he lived next door to her and they had grown up together, although they went to different schools now, he to the local all-boys school and she to the local all-girls. Those who did not know the pair well presumed they were boyfriend and girlfriend because they were inseparable but to be honest they had only ever been friends, albeit very good friends.

"Whatcha doin?" Aaron's way of a greeting.

"Nothing much, what about you?" Fidelma said as she stood up to put the catalogue away.

"Ah, not that long into the summer holidays and I'm bored already" yawned Aaron.

Fidelma laughed "how come when we were little we were never bored during the school holidays?"

Aaron laughed now too "because even if it was raining we would be outside playing, there always seemed to be so much to do, I supposed we used our imaginations then"

"Yeah we don't do that anymore" smiled Fidelma "it's not cool"

They laughed as they went into the kitchen to make some tea and raid the bickie jar, something that had become a tradition in both of their homes.

Fidelmas Mother came in, "You gonna come for dinner with us Saturday week Aaron?"

Aaron was surprised "Fidelmas birthday dinner? I thought that was family only?"

"Ah sure since when have you not been part of this family Aaron Murphy? Sure I have to think of you too when I'm doing the grocery shopping" said Fidelmas Mother playfully.

Aaron laughed "ah that's grand so Mrs Doyle thanks I'd love to go, you know me I never say no to a free feed. So Fiddles" he turned to Fidelma "what do you want for your birthday? 16 is kinda big isn't it? Will a voucher be too thoughtless"?

Fidelma laughed at this "Go on outta that Murphy, don't try and pretend that you ever pick my presents, I know your Mam always chooses them, you're such a bloke"

"Eh I'd like to think so" Aaron joked as he popped a biscuit into his mouth.

"Hey Mam, how come you and Dad haven't asked me what I'd like yet?" enquired Fidelma "time's running out ye know"

"Oh don't worry" said Mrs Doyle "we already know what we're getting you" and she smiled as she walked out of the kitchen.

Chapter 3:

Fidelmas 16th

Fidelma was so happy, she had had a great day with her friends, herself and 4 of her girlfriends went to the Cinema to see the latest Romcom, then

Aaron joined them afterwards for bowling. The craic was good and she got some lovely presents from the girls, she could not wait now for her night out, dinner with Aaron, her parents and brother Sean and then they were being joined by some of her Aunties, Uncles and cousins for a bit of a party back at the house, she loved that, although the last time they had all been together was Grannys months mind but she was going to try her best not to get upset tonight even though she wished with all her heart that her Granny would be with them, this was her first birthday without her and it was going to be so hard.

Fidelma went in the car with her parents and Aaron to the restaurant, they were meeting her brother Sean there, he was 20 and making his way there after work. The restaurant was buzzing when they arrived, they were seated straightway at a table by the window overlooking the river Liffey which was lovely at night because it did not matter if the river was clean or dirty, it was lit up beautifully and the streets were buzzing with people. After dinner they ordered desserts and Fidelmas was brought out with a sparkler in it and they all sang Happy Birthday, she was mortified but very delighted. Then it was time for presents, her favourite part, she was giddy with excitement. Sean went first, he handed Fidelma a card which she was very impressed with, usually he just handed her money, inside the card were two tickets to go and see her favourite band "Wow Sean" she squealed "that's fantastic!!! Thank you so much! Oh Aaron look! Aren't these brilliant?! I'm taking you with me, we'll have a ball"

Next it was Aarons turn, he handed her a card and a gift wrapped perfectly with bright pink wrapping paper and a shiny silver bow and ribbon "Oh Aaron, this card is beautiful" Fidelma cried as she read the card, it was much more mushy than the usual funny cards he had given her in the past "and I almost don't want to open the present it looks so perfect" but she carefully tore at the paper to reveal an expensive looking bottle of perfume. "Aaron! I'm speechless! Thank you this must've cost you a fortune, I love it" she said and as she leaned over to give him a hug and kiss on the cheek she felt the dynamics of their relationship shift suddenly, but it was nice and Aaron looked very chuffed with himself, if a little embarrassed.

"Ok" declared Fidelma as she adjusted her hair "time for the big parent pressie!"

"Fidelma" started her Mother "We are so proud of you. You're growing into a beautiful young lady"

"Mam!" Exclaimed Fidelma, she was mortified.

Fidelmas Dad laughed "Fidelma, I think what your Mother is trying to say is that we love you"

"Yes sweetheart" said her Mother "Happy 16th Birthday" and she handed Fidelma a dainty black velvet box.

Fidelma opened it very carefully, inside was a beautiful gold love heart locket charm, before she could speak her Mother handed her another little box and said with a wobble to her voice "and this is from Granny Fidelma."

Fidelma slowly took the box from her Mother and looked at it for a moment before carefully opening it, she was almost afraid to think what it might be in case she was wrong, but as she opened the box she caught her breath, it was Granny Fidelmas beloved charm bracelet, she had a few seconds of blinking before tears flowed freely and silently, her Mother came over and took Fidelma in her arms "Oh Fidelma darling, your Granny wanted you to have it for your sixteenth that's why I didn't say anything to you, Granny loved you very very much. Now let's put on your new charm and get that bracelet on your wrist where it belongs."

Well it was just the best night ever and with the charm bracelet on her wrist Fidelma felt as though her Granny was there too. They partied back at her parents' house with the rest of the family till the small hours, it was perfect.

Chapter 4:

And so it begins:

Fidelma woke very early the morning after the party, far too early for her liking, she had been looking forward to sleeping in till noon and had gone to bed earlier than some at around 2am but for some reason here she was lying wide awake at 6:30 in the morning. Fidelma lay in the bed for a while staring at the ceiling thinking over the past 24 hours or so, it had been a perfect birthday all except of course that Granny Fidelma was not there but having her charm bracelet meant so much to Fidelma, she reached over to her locker and picked it up, she examined each pretty charm until she came to one that she hadn't noticed before, a tiny weathered looking key, it was odd because it just looked so out of place, she fingered it for a few minutes until a sudden thought came to her, the treasure chest! Fidelma jumped out of bed and picked it up from her dressing table before nestling it in her lap as she sat on her bed. She looked at it for a moment, then with trembling hands she inserted the tiny key into the lock, it turned easily with a little click,

Fidelma didn't know what she was expecting but her heart was pounding, she figured it must be something extremely special for Granny to keep it locked at all times and carry the key around with her 24 hours a day. Fidelma suddenly hesitated, maybe she was not supposed to open it, but then she thought if that was the case Granny would have removed the key from the bracelet. No, she thought, she was definitely meant to open it.

It happened so fast, like lightening, a tiny ball of light flashed out from the chest, knocking it from Fidelmas grip, it seemed to bounce about the room for a moment before settling on the bed beside her. Fidelma stared, she must be dreaming, surely! She pinched herself, ouch; she felt that, oh my goodness was this really happening? There on the bed in front of her staring back in as much shock as herself, was what she could only describe as, a Fairy!

"Fidelma"? The creature spoke in the most beautiful voice.

Fidelma could not answer all she could do was stare with her mouth wide open.

It spoke again "Fidelma, what's happening? Why are you young again?

You look different; this isn't your home, what's going on?"

Fidelma could not believe she was answering the creature but she was going to go along with it anyway, "My name *is* Fidelma, but so was my Grannys, I'm her Granddaughter, Granny Fidelma passed away a couple of months ago"

The creature stared for a moment before tears began to silently stream down her face.

"Oh please don't be sad" comforted Fidelma, "She had a fantastic life and she lived to a great age, she said she didn't want anyone to cry when she left, but I know how you feel, I cried for a long time, I still do sometimes, I miss her so much"

There was silence for a moment, and then the creature spoke again, "Did she leave you the key and chest?"

"Yes" replied Fidelma "Yes she did"

"Well then" spoke the creature "that's that then, you are to take her place, it's what happens. I'm very pleased to meet you young Fidelma, I am Fairy Áine, Queen of the Fairies" and Fairy Áine extended her hand.

Fidelma took the tiny hand and shook it gently, she couldn't believe what was happening but at the same time she could believe it, suddenly everything about Granny was starting to make sense. But what did it mean for Fidelma now? What did Fairy Áine expect from her? Friendship? Would the fairy live in her bedroom in the chest? Could she tell anyone? No wait, of course she couldn't tell anyone, nobody in their right mind would believe her, oh she had so many questions for this little fairy, but apparently there was no time for questions.

Fairy Áine extended her tiny hand again and said "Ok Fidelma, let's do this", Fidelma took the Fairys hand and in a flash of lights and butterflies in her tummy she felt herself being whisked away from life as she knew it.

Chapter 5:

Fidelma could not believe her eyes, it still looked like Ireland but it was different, like something from an old fairy-tale, luscious green hills surrounded her, dotted with tiny stone cottages and in the distance what looked like a castle. They were standing in what Fidelma presumed was a fairy ring, her Granny had pointed them out to her before only now she was standing in it and feeling like she had walked under a ladder. Fidelma looked at Fairy Áine who was fluttering at her shoulder and as if reading Fidelmas mind the fairy simply said "No it's ok because I brought you into it." to which Fidelma simply nodded; she was still in complete shock and disbelief. Fairy Áine gestured towards a massive Oak tree, "Come" she said "come meet the clán." Fidelma looked at her in puzzlement, "Come to where?" she asked "It's a tree!" "No" said Fairy Áine "this is An crann darach Sean, this is our home. Come, follow me"

Fairy Áine flew to the base of the tree and opened a tiny door that Fidelma hadn't even noticed, "Tar isteach Fidelma, come inside." Fidelma was feeling very confused she reckoned she would be lucky if she could fit her hand through the tiny door but before she could answer, Fairy Áine flew up and took her by the hand, suddenly there were more flashes of light and Fidelma closed her eyes tight with dizziness, the next thing Fidelma knew she was inside the tree, except it was like a great big house carved from a tree trunk. It was the most amazing sight she had ever seen, and it was full of fairies busy doing their thing, well she presumed they were fairies because just like Fairy Áine, their faces all bore the same pointy features and they all had wings except they were all regular size like Fidelma, she realised quickly that the one beside her actually was Fairy Áine. "Oh" she gasped "you're big now, like me!"

"Silly" laughed Fairy Áine "I'm still the same size Cailín, it's you who's now the same size as me!" She laughed at Fidelmas puzzled face "well how else do you expect to fit inside An crann darach Sean? This is where I live with my fairy clán, now come and I'll introduce you they've been waiting to meet with you!"

Fidelma walked about shaking hands with all these beautiful creatures feeling like she was in a dream, yet she knew it was real. "So" said Fairy Áine "This is where my fairy clan live, there is so much for you to learn Fidelma and it's very important that you pay attention, this isn't the adventures of Tinkerbell, it's all very serious. Your job is to protect us and our land, as your Grandmother did and her Grandmother before her and so on." Fidelma stared at Fairy Áine for a moment before she spoke, "Protect you? I . . . I don't understand" she stammered "what do you need protection from?" Fairy Áine turned to face Fidelma "Oh" she said dramatically "everything young Fidelma, everything".

Fairy Áine proceeded to give Fidelma a tour of the Old Oak Tree, it was like nothing Fidelma had ever seen, at least not in real life, it reminded her of images she had conjured up in her mind as a child whilst listening to tales from her Granny, she had to pinch herself again to believe that here she was walking through room after room of fairies, busy making tools, furniture, food and general day to day objects, it was fascinating.

Eventually they sat down at a little wooden table and Fairy Áine began;

"Fidelma, you come from a long line of Friends of the Fairies, your Grandmother, her Grandmother and so on. It is a very important role but you must promise to be loyal to us, and trust us as we will be trusting of you. This might seem like a strange land to you but it is in fact Ireland, old Ireland really but it lives on separately from the Ireland that you know. Thousands of years ago, Ireland was a Mythical land, but foreign people start arriving at our shores in big ships, and they didn't understand our ways, our customs and traditions, they had ways of their own, and were fearful of our magic so slowly but surely things started to change, then gradually there was a split, and now old Ireland and the new age Ireland that you know, carry on in parallel universes, and you mo chara, can travel between both, a unique gift bestowed upon you, but you must use it wisely and for the greater good of our beautiful land."

Fidelma sat looking at Fairy Áine, eyes wide, she could not believe what she was hearing, she had so many questions. "So" she started "did you take Granny Fidelma here too when she was my age?" Fairy Áine smiled fondly "Yes Fidelma I did and we had some great times together, she was so feisty and loyal and such a fast learner." Fidelma looked puzzled "A fast learner? What did she need to learn?" she asked completely in awe. Fairy Áine closed her hands over Fidelmas hands on the table "Fidelma, we had to teach her everything that we will also be teaching you, and possibly we will need to teach you some extra things too, life is fast changing in your world, people barely use pen and paper anymore." Before Fidelma could answer Fairy Áine continued, producing some paper and a quill with a little jar of ink, Fidelma was transfixed on the fluid movement of the quill in the fairy's dainty hands. "Now" she continued "I'm preparing a list of your training, you needn't worry about time, 24 hours here is one minute in your new land so you will come here for all your training. Now I have a few questions, do you play any instruments?" Fidelma was thrown by this question. "Eh, yes" she replied "I've been playing the tin whistle since I was 6 and started the Fiddle when I was 9 and still play both, I have quite a few trophies and medals for playing them in the Fleadh Cheoil." she finished proudly. Fairy Áine looked up at her for a moment and said "Excellent, you will need some harp lessons so."

Fairy Áine spent about an hour writing her list, asking questions and chatting to other fairies, she asked Fidelma many questions, even what weapons or tools Fidelma was familiar with using and tut tutted when Fidelma could not think of any.

Finally the list was finished; she rolled it into a scroll securing it with a piece of twine and handed it to Fidelma, "keep this safe" she said "now, let's eat!"

Fidelma was escorted into the biggest room in the tree house where a massive banquet was laid out on a long table, fairies stood around silently staring at her as she walked into the room with Fairy Áine by her side, they waited until Fairy Áine gave the nod and then they all began tucking into the food spread out on the table. An extra dainty fairy approached Fidelma with a little wooden plate and offered it to her "Here" she said "fill your plate." Fidelma smiled and did just that, it was a tremendous feast and she eventually felt herself relax and feel strangely at home among the fairies as they chatted excitedly with her. She began imagining what it must have been like for her Granny when she first came here, she wondered was she scared? Excited? Or just completely bewildered like she was feeling! As the feast came to an end, a trio of fairies appeared, two with fiddles and one with a tin whistle and they began to play a reel to which everyone else started to dance to and eventually Fidelma joined in too, it was such fun and she was sad when she heard a fairy blow on a horn which obviously signified the festivities had come to an end.

Fairy Áine now approached her again "Come Fidelma, it is time for you to go back to your world for now, have a good rest for this trip takes a lot out of you, and have a read over your list but remember to keep it very safe. I will be back for you again tomorrow just as the sun is setting in your world so make sure you are in your bedroom." She put out her hand

and led Fidelma back outside and into the fairy ring and once again in a flash of light and butterflies in her tummy, Fidelma was transported back to her bedroom. She was back sitting on her bed with the treasure chest in her lap and Fairy Áine fluttering beside her. "Ok Fidelma" whispered the fairy "it's time for me to go, I will see you soon. Remember, as the sun is setting. Be safe" and with that she fluttered up right in front of Fidelmas face where she planted the most delicate kiss on her forehead and in a flash of colourful lights she was gone.

Fidelma sat on the bed for what felt like an eternity, she was trying to process what had just happened, she looked at her bedside clock, it read 6:50am, she decided to climb back under the covers and get some rest just as she was asked, in no time Fidelma was fast asleep, dreaming of a land of fairies.

Chapter 6:

It was almost noon when Fidelma woke to a gentle knocking on her bedroom door and her Mother softly calling her "Fidelma, Fidelma love are you awake?"

Slowly the door opened, and her Mother popped her head in "Ah you're awake love, are you ok?" She asked as she came and sat on the bed "It was a long day for you yesterday, did you enjoy it?" Fidelma smiled up at her Mother "Oh Mam it was just the best birthday ever thank you so much" and she squeezed her Mother tightly, when they broke away her Mother noticed Fidelmas face was wet with tears "Fidelma love" she exclaimed "what is it? Is something wrong?" Fidelma gave a watery smile "ah no Mam I think I'm just overwhelmed and what have ye" she paused for a minute "and I miss Granny!" And there it was, the wobble, followed by tears flowing freely, her Mother just put her arms around her and held her tightly, and for a few minutes they sat like that, rocking gently and silently.

Meanwhile in the treasure chest on the dresser, Fairy Áine was inside looking out the keyhole at the emotional scene, she felt a tear run down her cheek which she swiftly wiped away with her hand.

"Ok" said Mrs Doyle as they both began wiping their eyes "Your Dad is downstairs making one of his famous fry ups so get yourself together and come down, a handful of the family stayed over last night, they're sprawled on couches and chairs and all sorts" she smiled "Come on, I'll stick the kettle on" Fidelma smiled at her Mother "Thanks Mam, I'll be down in a minute, you go on ahead." As soon as she heard her Mothers footsteps on the stairs Fidelma reached under her bed and produced the scroll Fairy Áine had given her. She unfurled it and held it out so she could read it

Always keep the two worlds separate
Be loyal to the Fairies

Don't speak of us to anyone from the New World

Study hard in Irish class

Learn and practise to sew

Learn how to shoot a bow and arrow

Work out and keep fit

Learn to write with a Quill

Meet with Cailte Mac Rónáin

Take Rowing lessons

Learn to ride a horse

Learn how to play the Harp

Fidelma stared at the scroll for a moment after she finished reading it, she just couldn't get her head round it, she was dumbfounded, "Learn how to shoot a bow and arrow?" she muttered to herself, "and who the heck is Caílte Mac Rónáin when he's at home?" Well, she thought as she rolled up the scroll again, she can ask all these questions and more this evening when Fairy Áine came back for her. She safely stowed the scroll under her bed and went downstairs to have some of that yummy breakfast she could smell.

Fidelma entered the busy kitchen, Dad was at the cooker singing away to himself, some Aunties and Uncles were sitting at the table with Fidelma's Mother chatting away, a couple of cousins were getting plates and things sorted and a couple of others were sitting at the counter holding their heads. Mrs. Doyle poured Fidelma a mug of tea from the pot on the table "Come on over love."

It was a lovely afternoon, relaxed and fun, everyone still in good form from the night before, there was plenty of chatting and laughing but Fidelma found it very hard to concentrate, she had so many things going around in her head and she kept looking at the clock, it seemed like it was going backwards. Eventually there was a knock on the door; it was Aaron so

Fidelma grabbed her hoody and headed out for a walk with her friend.

"So" said Aaron "had you a good birthday?"

"I had the best birthday ever" said Fidelma

"Right, that's good, you seem a bit distracted though, is everything ok?" he asked.

"ah I'm just exhausted" lied Fidelma, but she couldn't help but think just how well Aaron knew her, she figured she was going to have to be careful around him from now on, try not to act suspicious 'keep the 2 worlds separate', jeez it's going to be so hard.

Later that evening Fidelma was sitting in the sitting room with her family watching TV, the sun was starting to go down, 'at last' she thought "I'm just going up to my room to read a book" she announced to no one in particular.

Once upstairs she closed her bedroom door and stood quietly for a moment just listening, making sure nobody else was coming up the stairs, then she picked up the treasure chest and sat down on her bed with it in her lap once again. She inserted the tiny key into the lock and turned it till it clicked and once again there was a flash of light as Fairy Áine popped out of the chest and came to land on the bed beside Fidelma "Well" she said "Breithlá Sona Fidelma, Happy Birthday" and fluttered up and kissed Fidelma gently on the forehead "Thank you" said Fidelma beaming.

Fairy Áine extended her hand and said "Ok Fidelma take my hand, there's something I'd like you to see, come" Fidelma took her hand and just like the last time she saw bright flashes of light and felt butterflies in her tummy, her eyes were shut tightly and when she opened them again she was in the fairy ring, she saw The Old Oak Tree and went to make towards it but fairy Áine stopped her, "No Fidelma there's something I want to show you first, there's great festivities today and I thought it would be special for you to go and see them"

Fidelma was excited "Oooh what sort of festivities?"

"Oh" started Fairy Áine "it's a wedding, King Lir is marrying Aoife"

"Oh my goodness" squealed Fidelma in excitement "A real royal wedding? Wow!"

"Yes" said Fairy Áine "but I'm guessing it's nothing like any Royal wedding you might've seen on your box in the New World, this is a wedding of the Thuatha Dé Danann"

Fidelma looked puzzled "who're the Thuatha Dé Danann?"

"They're supernaturally gifted people; they're very important around here and must never be crossed. Although King Lir is a kind King and his people love him, they were very saddened for him when his first wife and love of his life Aoibh died, he was terribly upset and if it wasn't for his beloved children who knows what would've become of him" explained Fairy Áine.

"Oh" said Fidelma "That's awful, how many children are there?"

"Four" said Fairy Áine "three boys Aodh, the twins; Fiachra and Conn and one girl Fionnuala, she is the eldest and is said to be the most beautiful creature."

"And who is he marrying now?" asked Fidelma as she walked along with Fairy Áine fluttering beside her

"Aoife, she is the sister of Aoibh, when Aoibh died, her Father, Bodb Derg decided that King Lir should take his other daughter as a wife and Mother to his grandchildren" explained the fairy.

"Oh" replied Fidelma "not really a typical fairy-tale romance is it?"

"I did tell you it would be different than what you are used to" answered Fairy Áine "Aoibh was a lovely woman who adored her children and I hope that Aoife can be the Mother that these lovely children need"

"You sound doubtful" said Fidelma

"Well, I get bad vibes from Aoife, like I said the Tuatha Dé Danann have magical powers, and mostly they're used for the greater good but sometimes if a person has a bit of wickedness in their heart then the powers can be dangerous"

After another few minutes they had arrived at a huge stone castle, it was like nothing Fidelma had ever seen, at least not in real life, it reminded her of drawings of old medieval castles she had seen in books, certainly nothing like she was expecting, she supposed she had watched too many Disney movies.

As they approached there were two guards in full suits of armour and what looked like spears and shields, blocking the main entrance. Fidelma felt her heart pounding in her chest; she suddenly wished she was back home in her bedroom, actually reading a book! Fairy Áine spoke to the guards, "Fairy Áine Queen of Fairies and my guest Fidelma, protector of Fairies" The guards bowed and stood apart to allow them to enter, Fidelma was shaking.

They entered a big stone hallway with tall candlesticks along the wall to give some light, Fidelma shuddered as she imagined what it would be like if the candles blew out. They followed the sound of music into a great

Ballroom, it was magnificent, it was decorated beautifully with flowers and candles for the occasion and in the corner were some musicians, there were chairs set up on either side of the room to create an aisle in the centre, Fairy Áine led Fidelma to a seat. She watched open mouthed as other people came and took their seats, all in their finery, it was like being part of a play seeing their old-style dress, so many different characters, Fidelma was amazed. At last a man took centre stage and called for silence, a hush fell over the crowd and the musicians struck up a melody, it was a beautiful haunting tune and Fidelma felt Goosebumps prickle her skin. Suddenly a tall man dressed head to toe in Royal finery and a gold crown walked up the aisle, he had such a presence about him, Fidelma could almost sense that he was a good man; he was in fact, King Lir. He took his place at the top of the room and turned to watch his bride to be walk up the aisle, accompanied by her father. Bodb Derg was an extremely large man but he had a kind face, beside him, his daughter Aoife was beautiful and her gown was magnificent but as she passed by Fidelma felt a shiver go down her spine, she did not give off good vibes and when King Lir lifted her veil and she turned to smile at the crowd her smile did not reach her vivid green eyes. Fidelma shifted uncomfortably in her seat, she now understood what Fairy Áine meant, she looked around the room until her eyes fell on 4 children seated at the front, 3 handsome boys and a very beautiful girl, Fidelma watched them as their Father married their Auntie, she could see in their faces that they were worried and her heart broke for them.

After the ceremony the guests were invited into another grand room, where the longest table Fidelma had ever seen was laden down with food, massive legs of ham circled a bigger plate in the centre which to Fidelmas horror contained none other than the head of a pig, "eugh gross" she muttered before she could stop herself, a man beside her turned his head sharply "what was that?" he asked "I said Go Hálainn" answered Fidelma quickly "It all just looks so beautiful" The man smiled and bowed his head, Fidelma felt a little flap against her ear "Mind what you say Fidelma" hissed Fairy Áine "Sorry, it slipped out" Fidelma answered sheepishly.

As magnificent as the feast on the table looked, when it came to eating it Fidemla soon realised it was very primitive and she quickly lost her appetite. Fairy Áine was mingling with some other fairies so Fidelma decided to explore a little, she left the grand room and found herself in a long hallway, once again the only light was coming from candles along the wall in tall candlesticks, there were a couple of what looked like Knights suits of armour on display, like something she had seen in the movies but to be honest in real life they were creepy, Fidelma half expected them to move as she tiptoed past them. There was daylight at the end of the long hallway to what looked like a garden, and that was where Fidelma was heading.

Fidelma squinted her eyes in the bright sunshine when she stepped outside, the garden looked magnificent, just so many different shades of green, there were Rose bushes on one side and apple trees on the other, but past the apple trees was a little stream and there sitting on a rock was the beautiful Fionnuala. Fidelma walked towards her and quietly sat down on a rock beside her "It was a beautiful ceremony" she began "You must be very happy for your Father" Fionnuala turned to face Fidelma, her face wet with tears "I am so incredibly scared"

"Why?" Fidelma asked, but Fionnualla just shook her head

"I'm sorry" she answered "I did not mean to say that, you took me by surprise, do I know you?"

"Oh please don't be sorry" began Fidelma extending her hand "My name is Fidelma, I'm the protector of Fairies!"

The two girls shook hands and sat in silence for a couple of minutes,

Fidelma was desperately trying to think of something to say, she guessed that Fionnuala was the same age as herself or close to it but she had no idea how to start a conversation with a teenager who had never seen a TV and wouldn't have a notion who U2 were, but in the end it was Fionnuala who broke the silence

"We lost our Mother three years ago, it was heart wrenching for myself and my brothers, but my Father, he too was heartbroken and Grandfather insisted he needed to take a new companion who could also be a Mother to us, and so it was arranged that Aunt Aoife would be the one"

Fidelma felt so sorry for the girl, being so close to her own Mother she couldn't imagine what she must have gone through "And why are you so scared Fionnuala, don't you love your Aunt Aoife?"

Fionnualas face went pale "She is a wicked wicked woman and has no love for me nor my brothers, she just pretends when Father or Grandfather are around, but when we are on our own with her she says cruel things, she says that Father loves her more than he ever loved our Mother and that soon his heart will fill with so much love for her that he will no longer have room in his heart for us" and with that she burst into tears.

Wow, Fidelma was baffled; didn't this girl understand that the heart can't fill up with love until it can't fit anymore in? "Jeez" thought Fidelma "they take things so literally here in the Old Ireland."

"Listen" began Fidelma cautiously "I can tell you for a fact that that is not how the heart works, it does not get full when you have too much love in it! That's the wonderful thing about it, you can love you parents and your Aunties and Uncles, your Grandparents and your own children and even your friends! Your Fathers heart is not going to run out of room for the love of his children! He loves you now and that's that! There is no changing that, whether he loves Aoife too, or not, you are his children, nothing can come between your love"

Fionnuala was listening to Fidelma wide eyed "Oh Fidelma" she cried "you are so wise!" and she threw her arms around her "I shall tell my brothers what you have told me, and we will see that our Father will always love us"

The two girls stood up "I must go back in" said Fionnuala

"Yes" agreed Fidelma "Me too, Fairy Áine will be wondering where I've got to, it was lovely to meet you"

"Oh you too Fidelma" gushed Fionnuala "It is so nice to have a friend to talk to about these things"

The girls walked companionably back through the dark hallway and into the Grand room where the festivities were in full swing, the dancing had started and it all looked like great fun to Fidelma, but as she stood there clapping along to the music she spotted the now 'Queen' Aoife, she had an icy stare as she watched King Lir dance around the grand room with his beautiful daughter, they both seemed so happy and carefree and yet Queen Aoifes cold eyes sent a shiver down Fidelmas spine.

"I know" whispered a familiar voice in Fidelmas ear "I feel it too" Fidelma was startled but relaxed when she realised it was Fairy Áine "That woman was born with a wicked heart and we are going to have to keep a close eye on those children"

Fairy Áine and Fidelma soon slipped away from the festivities and made their way back to the Old Oak Tree where once again Fidelma was brought inside.

"Come sit" motioned Fairy Áine to a bench at a table "have some tea, we have so much to discuss"

Chapter 7

It was a beautiful Summers Day in Dublin and Fidelma and Aaron were in the City Centre, Fidelma was clothes shopping and Aaron was looking for a good pair of runners so they had spilt up and agreed to meet back for lunch in St. Stephens Green, a large park at the top end of Grafton Street.

Aaron was sitting on a park bench with his one bag containing his runners sitting at his feet, he laughed when he spotted Fidelma approach with her five bags swinging at her sides. When she arrived at their meeting point they both held up their O'Briens Sandwich Bar brown paper bags and said "Snap".

They sat companionably eating and chatting and enjoying their afternoon people watching, St Stephens Green is always busy on days like this, it was full of local shop workers catching some rays of sunshine on their lunch break and shoppers just enjoying the break from the hustle and bustle of the shops. "Did you know" started Aaron "that during the 1916 Rising, shooting was temporarily halted to allow the groundsman for this park feed the ducks?" Fidelma looked at him for a moment, she never knew if he was messing or serious, Aaron recognised her look, "Seriously!" he exclaimed, slightly affronted that she might not believe him. "Really?" asked Fidelma "wow you are a fountain of knowledge Aaron Murphy, speaking of which, let's go feed the ducks"

The pair wandered through the park chatting until they reached the big lake which was home to many ducks, Fidelma began breaking up the crusts from her sandwich which she never ate, "We should go look at some of the monuments" said Aaron, obviously already bored with the ducks "Can we wait until we see some swans first please?" answered Fidelma in a small voice adding "You're obsessed with history, last time we were here you took me to see the bust of Constance Markievicz and gave me a run down on her life" "Yeah" said Aaron "But Fidelma our country is soaked with history, it's amazing! Don't you ever wish you could take a step back in time and see what Ireland was like in the olden days?" Fidelma stared at him for a moment, oh poor Aaron, she thought, he would love to have seen even a snippet of what she had seen so far, she was considering how to answer him without giving anything away when her thoughts were interrupted by the arrival of some swans looking for their share of the bread "Oh look" squealed Fidelma "Aaron look at the swans aren't they beautiful? They're so majestic; I could watch them all day!" "Okay" conceded Aaron "stay with the swans for a while so and then we'll look at the monuments" Fidelma smiled in reply, she loved the swans.

Later that evening when Fidelma finished her dinner she helped her Mother stack the dishwasher and clean up before she retreated to her room. She unlocked the Treasure Chest and sat on her bed, she smiled thinking of the lovely day she had, she was thinking of the swans when the chest popped open and out flew the little flash of light, Fidelma felt herself getting excited but her face fell when she seen Fairy Áines expression, it was one of anguish "Quickly Fidelma" she said "you must come at once, something terrible has happened".

Chapter 8

They were sitting in An Crann darach Sean, Fairy Áine was busy drawing up a map, when she was finished she spoke "Fidelma, our worst fears have been confirmed" Fidelma felt a shiver go down her spine, straight away she thought of the beautiful Fionnuala and her handsome brothers, "Not the Children of King Lír?" she asked, Fairy Áine simply bowed her head in reply.

"Two days ago" began the fairy "Aoife said she was taking the children to visit her Father, Bodb Derg, when they reached Lough Derravaragh she stopped the chariot and being such a beautiful summers day told the children they could have a swim in the lake to cool down" Fairy Áine paused to take a sip from her little cup, clearly shaken, Fidelma was franticly imagining allsorts, Fairy Áine continued "When the children were in the water Aoife produced her rowan wand and changed the children into swans!" Fidelma gasped at the little fairy "Swans?" she questioned "what? Why? I don't understand!" Fairy Áine put her hand on Fidelmas shoulder and spoke again "She is a wicked woman is Aoife, as she made her spell she called 'Be as swans here on Lough Derravaragh for three hundred years and then for another three hundred years on the sea of Moyle, after that you will spend three hundred years on the Western Ocean. You will remain as swans for all of those years or until a time when the Man from the North will join the Woman from the South' she then told them she would leave them their gift of voice, they are still able to speak with human voices but that is all Fidelma."

To say Fidelma was shocked would be an understatement, and if she was honest, she was also a little frightened, what had she gotten herself involved in? How on earth was she meant to help the children of King Lir? She had no magic! All of these thoughts were going through Fidelmas head, Fairy Áine looked at her "Fidelma, this is no time for panic my dear, these children need us, we will go to see their Father and then to the lake to see the children"

Fidelma stepped outside the Oak Tree with Fairy Áine to an image she never thought she would see; 3 fairies preparing what looked like a saddle on the back of a grey hare, she looked at her fairy friend questioningly "This is our transport Fidelma" said Fairy Áine, "that is why I have kept you fairy size! Now, climb aboard Fidelma" gestured Fairy Áine and Fidelma climbed to the back of the saddle with the help of the other fairies while Fairy Áine seated herself at the front and took the reins.

They seemed to have been travelling for an age but Fidelma was enjoying the beautiful countryside and extremely fresh air, after a while Fairy Áine brought the hare to a stop and they both climbed down from the saddle.

"Stretch your legs young Fidelma" said Fairy Áine "we will stop a while here and have a bite to eat so Eimhin can have some rest, he is fast but this is a long journey for him with us on his back"

Fidelma wandered about stretching her legs and arms, amazed at the massive daisies and buttercups that surrounded her, she walked to a daisy that was about the same height as herself and touched its pretty petals, "Wow" she exclaimed "I didn't realise they grew so big, they're like, daisy trees!"

Fairy Áine laughed "Oh Fidelma dear, you're still fairy size, remember?" she said putting her hand to her mouth as she giggled, Fidelma laughed now too "Of course" she giggled "Everything that I see and do here is so completely unreal to me that I didn't even question the fact that I was sitting on the back of a rabbit racing through fields of grass that seemed as high as a house" With that, Eibhin gave a little snuffle, Fairy Áine giggled some more "Not a rabbit Fidelma dear, a hare, Eimhin has been our main form of transport for some time now" Fairy Áine spoke as she opened up a satchel and produced a canteen of water and a cloth pouch which contained bread and cheese, then from the saddle she took out a small blanket and spread it on the ground "Come Fidelma, sit and eat"

Fidelma actually enjoyed the snack as she had been feeling quiet peckish, it was a beautiful afternoon, and the sun was high in the sky. "So" said Fidelma, munching on her bread "Does Eimhins name have a meaning?" "Oh yes" replied Fairy Áine "All names have meanings, and Eimhin means swift, because, well, he is very swift" They both smiled and looked over at Eimhin who was busy grazing on the grass "but" continued Fairy Áine "As swift as he may be, he is no match for a horse, unfortunately, we are too tiny to ride a horse, but you on the other hand Fidelma, you would be perfect, so that is one of the first things you are going to need lessons in" Fidelma gulped, wow, horse riding? Who'd have thought!

It was time to continue on their journey, Fairy Áine assured Fidelma they didn't have too much father to go. Fidelma was ejoying the journey, they had come to what seemed to be a village, where there were numerous little stone cottages and, in the distance, a castle, Fairy Áine explained though that it was actually a Kingdom, and the castle was where they were heading, to meet King Lír. "Wasn't that the Kings castle we were in for the wedding though?" asked Fidelma. "No" replied Fairy Áine "That castle belongs to some Monks and some of the more significant ceremonies are performed there." Fidelma took this in; she was constantly feeling there was more for her to learn than simply what was written on the scroll.

# Chapter 9

They eventually arrived at the castle, Fidelma looked up in awe, she had quite literally never seen a sight like it. The castle was enormous and stood proudly at the top of a hill, it was surrounded by beautiful trees and flowers, the building itself was tall with 5 turrets sprouting out from the main part, but what caught Fidelmas eye was the fact that on such a beautiful sunny day the castle was shadowed by a dark grey cloud dispensing hazy rain. Fairy Áine noticed Fidelma's bewildered expression and explained "Here Fidelma, you can literally see, feel or often hear emotion if it is strong enough, this darkened cloud represents King Lír's broken heart, it is an extremely sad time. I have been to this castle many times and only after the death of the lovely Aoibh did I witness such thunderous heartache, we must proceed cautiously as the King will be very delicate, but worry not as he *is* expecting us, after all, it was the King himself who sent for us for he believes only **we** can help solve this dreadful situation" Fidelma stared at Fairy Áine for a moment, she wasn't sure which scared her more, the thunderous cloud that represented the Kings heartache or the word 'we'!

Before they proceded Fairy Áine flew around Fidelma like a whirlwind and when she stopped Fidelma found herself back to her original size, Fairy Áine fluttered in front of her with her hands on her hips and a frown on her face as she looked Fidelma up and down.

"What is it?" asked Fidelma.

"It's the clothes" replied Fairy Áine, "we will have to change the clothes for this meeting with King Lír if he is to take you seriously at all, you look like you have arrived from another planet" Fidelma felt slightly affronted, she loved her comfy Adidas track pants but she could see the little fairy had a point so she simply nodded and with that once again Fairy Áine flew around her like a whirlwind and when she stopped Fidelma looked down to find herself totally transformed, she was wearing boots with extremely coarse brown pants tucked into them, a slightly ruffled top and an open waistcoat, she felt strangely like a pirate and stifled a giggle as she imagined what Aaron would say if he saw her looking like this. Fairy Áine soon reminded Fidelma that this was no laughing matter though as she wagged her finger "Fidelma you need to fit in and these clothes are perfect for travel and whatever else you might need to undertake." The entrance to the castle was flanked by guards in similar amour as the last ones Fidelma had seen; as they approached Fidelma could feel the hairs stand on the back of her neck, such an eeriness she had never felt before. The guards looked at Fidelma and then to Fairy Áine, they bowed to the fairy and stood aside to let them pass through the massive doorway.

Once inside the castle, Fidelma could literally feel the sorrow, she couldn't explain it but she could definitely feel it, she walked slowly following Fairy Áine through a long dark corridor, lit only by the odd candle. At the end of the corridor was a big wooden door "You will need to knock Fidelma for my knock will not be heard" said Fairy Áine. Fidelma looked back at the Fairy, terrified, she just wanted to be back in her bedroom, but Fairy Áine nodded to her in encouragement so Fidelma clenched her fist and gave a knock on the hard wood. They stood in silence for what felt like an eternity but was only half a minute or so, Fidelma was wondering if Fairy Áine could hear her teeth chatter when she heard a mans voice from the other side of the door "Come in!"

Fidelma pushed open the heavy door and Fairy Áine flew in before her as they entered an enormous room, it was also dark but with slightly more light than the hallway, in the centre of the room was a massive table that would seat 18 people, but only one seat was occupied, sitting slumped in the large chair at the head of the table was a grief stricken King Lir. Fidelma cast her mind back to the magnificent ceremony that was the Royal Wedding, she recalled that on that occasion she felt that King Lir was a man of such immense presence, he gave off a strong aura of being a good strong man, but looking at him here hunched at the table he was almost unrecognizable, he looked, she searched her brain to find a word that would perfectly sum up the man she saw before her, broken! He looked broken.

King Lir did not look up as they entered the room; Fairy Áine looked at Fidelma before clearing her throat to speak "King Lir, you sent for us?" Slowly the King looked up at his two guests, his eyes were raw from crying, it seemed to take him a moment to register who stood before him and then he gestured for them to sit at the table. Fidelma slowly walked over and took a seat close to the King, Fairy Áine sat on the table between the two. The King spoke first "She took my children from me Fairy Áine, I trusted her" Fairy Áine simply nodded and King Lir started to sob, Fidelma could feel the hair stand on her neck again, this was going to be an extremely hard conversation.

Fairy Áine spoke after a moment "King Lir can you tell us what happened, start from the beginning, take your time" King Lir took a moment to compose himself before he proceeded with his sorrowful tale;

Aoife told me one morning that she intended to take the children to see their Grandfather Bodb Derg, I saw nothing wrong with this as Bodh loves the children as they do him, she said she would be back the following morning. It is a long journey you see so they would need to stay overnight but the following morning there was no sign of them, by afternoon I stood on the hill waiting for sight of the carriage, I was beginning to worry, before the sun began to set I caught sight of the carriage in the distance and I breathed a sigh of relief. I went back into the castle and waited for them to come through the door, waited for my children to run to me and excitedly great me as they had done many times before, but they did not come, instead it was Aoife who appeared through the door, she was crying, she said there had been an accident and that the children had been fatally injured and could not be saved, but I saw something in her eyes, something I have never witnessed before because had I seen what I seen that day I would never have married

Aoife, as the sister of my lovely Aoibh is of evil heart. I ran at her and demanded that she tell me the truth about my beautiful children, she laughed and said she had used her magic to turn them into swans, they will spend 300 years on Lake Derravaragh, 300 years on Straits of Moyle and 300 years on the Isle of Inish Glora, the enchantment can only be broken when the man from the North joins the woman from the South. I was furious; I lashed out and banished her from my Kingdom. I hear she fled to her Fathers Kingdom.

Fidelma was shocked, this was just unreal, those poor beautiful children, but it was Fairy Áine who spoke; "Have you seen the children?" King Lir looked at Fairy Áine before he answered "This is the first time I have returned to the castle, to meet you, I have spent every passing second down at Lake Derravaragh with my beloved children, I have slept on the shore the past two nights. My children can still speak, they are holding up well, Fionuala is being very brave, she has become very protective of Aodh and the twins, I told her she is so like her Mother" and with this he began to cry again, he wiped at his eyes before he continued "Can you help me? Can you break the enchantment so my children are not left as swans for 900 years?"

Fidelma wasn't so sure, she just could not imagine what she could possibly do to help, however she hoped Fairy Áine would be able to use her magic to break the spell, she watched the Fairy as she gave her reply "Believe me when I tell you King Lir we will do our upmost to help, but you do understand that my magic is no match for that of the Tuatha Dé Danann, however we will do whatever we can to end the enchantment"

Fidelma was full of questions and was eager to learn as much as she could about the evil Aoife, she addressed the King carefully as she spoke up "King Lir, can you tell me why you think Aoife has done this to your children?"

King Lir thought for a moment before he answered "Aoife was of jealous heart, I should have seen it before, the signs were there but I ignored them" he looked Fidelma in the eye "I never imagined she would hurt the children, but one of my servants has since come to the castle to tell me that Aoife ordered him to take the children to the forest the day before and kill them but when he refused she banished him from the castle and told him if he ever returned or told me of her request she would have him killed and his children turned into wild boars"

Fidelma was horrified by this but she knew she must thread carefully with her next question "So if her original plan was to have the children killed, why then do you think she changed them into swans, thus sparing their lives?"

Fairy Áine began with some of the answer "The Tuatha Dé Danann", Fidelma looked at the Fairy puzzled and King

Lir gave the rest of the answer "Aoife knew that if she herself took the children's lives, then their ghosts would haunt her, forever!"

Fidelma nodded "ok" she thought for a moment then posed her next question "Why swans though? She threatened to change the servants' children into wild boars, why did she choose swans for your children?"

Again Fairy Áine supplied part of the answer by saying simply "She didn't" Fidelma was puzzled yet again "Hmmm?" was all she could manage looking from the Fairy to the King, it was the King who supplied the rest of the information "She didn't *choose* to turn them into swans, she might have suggested any animal or bird but because I their Father am King Lir, Ruler of the Sea they would have taken on the form most closely associated with their heritage"

"I see" said Fidelma, though she wondered did she and also, how she was staying so calm in such a bizarre situation she had no idea.

Fairy Áine stood up suddenly and fluttered her wings "King Lir we must leave now, but I give you my word we will be in touch soon" She extended her tiny hand, the King opened his huge hand and Fairy Áine placed her little hand, palm down onto his open palm, they closed their eyes for a moment before breaking away, the King then extended his hand to Fidelma who shook his hand warmly and the unlikely pair made their way out of the room, down the long dark corridor out into the fresh air.

Fidelma blinked in the daylight, her eyes adjusting after being in the darkness of the castle. "You done well Fidelma" said Fairy Áine approvingly "You asked good questions" she spoke as the pair walked to where Eimhin was waiting patiently "Now, unfortunately, is the dangerous part" Fidelma looked at the fairy aghast "Dangerous?" Fairy Áine began adjusting the saddle on the hare, she turned to Fidelma "We must now go see Bodh Derg, we do not know if Aoife is still with him, although if I know Bodh, he will have banished her from his own Kingdom but if not, our visit could mean danger, are you up to it?" Without taking a moment to think about it Fidelma answered "Of course" Fairy Áine smiled "Good" she said "now, climb aboard".

As Eimhin ran through the fields, Fairy Áine seated at the front of the saddle holding the reins and Fidelma sitting behind her holding on tight she thought about the children, now beautiful swans, swimming on the Lake Derravaragh as they speak to their heartbroken Father on the shore, she thought about the swans she had seen in St. Stephens Green with Aaron and realised that felt like a lifetime ago, she thought of her parents and all they do for her to keep her safe and happy and she thought of her Granny, she felt her eyes well up with unexpected tears as she felt deep in her gut that she must do whatever she can to save the Children of Lir.

Chapter 10

They travelled this time without stopping, so when Eimhin finally did come to a stop Fidelma was relieved but confused when she realised they had stopped at the Crann darach Sean, Fairy Áine climbed down first and a bewildered Fidemla followed "Em" started Fidelma "I thought we were going to Bodh Deargs?" Fairy Áine looked taken aback as she answered "Oh my dear Fidelma, we cannot go straight there, we have much preparation to do beforehand, for as I said, we do not know what danger might await us. No, you will go home and get some rest, sleep well tonight, in the morning I will come back for you as the sun is rising, you will come back here for some horse riding lessons, we will have to do that in a day, then you will come back and have some lessons in archery, you will need another good nights rest then before you come back and meet with Cailte Mac Ronain, you will need your wits about you before you meet with him and then we can head off to Bodh Deargs Kingdom"

Fidelma was helping Fairy Áine take the saddle off Eimhin as she was talking but she was dumbfounded "I don't understand" she said "I thought it was urgent that we solve this for King Lir and save the children? It sounds to me like it will be at least another 4 days before we get to Bodh Deargs?"

Fairy Áine patted the rump of Eimhin and he went on his way, she took Fidelmas hand and they walked towards the Crann darach Sean "Fidelma" she spoke "Remember the list I gave you?" Fidelma nodded and the Fairy continued "Well I thought we would have a week or two to get through that list before we got to work but Aoife has changed that, however, those children are destined to be swans for 900 years, 4 days is not going to matter that much" She walked to the fire and hung a pot of water over it for tea "Fidelma" she continued "we need to be prepared, you are here to help us but you cannot do that without the proper skills, do you understand?" Fidelma was overwhelmed and answered quietly "Yes." "Besides" continued Fairy Áine "it would take us forever to get to Bodh Deargs Kingdom on Eimhins back, we need to go by horse. Tea?" Fidelma nodded and took a seat at the table, she stared ahead of her as fairies busied around her, suddenly she was feeling the effects of their day, she was so tired she closed her eyes for a moment. Fairy

Áine approached the table with the two mugs of steaming hot tea, she stopped when she realised Fidelma had her eyes closed, she stood and watched her for a moment, she put the mugs down on the table and placed a hand on Fidelmas shoulder, making her open her eyes with a start "I wasn't sleeping" protested Fidelma. "It's ok Fidelma" said Fairy Áine soothingly, taking a seat beside her "You must be exhausted, it has been a long and emotional day and it takes its toll, here have some sweet tea"

Fidelma cupped the hot mug and gratefully sipped the sweet drink, she savoured each mouthful, finding it strangely comforting, it reminded her, she realised of tea her Granny used to make her. Fairy Áine extended her hand and placed it over Fidelmas hand "Tomorrow is another day young Fidelma" she said, Fidelma smiled at her, she was suddenly glad that they had not gone straight to Bodh Deargs kingdom, she ached for her bed. Fairy Áine continued "I will come for you in the morning as I said, so be up and dressed, you can have some breakfast here and then we will start with the horse riding lessons so make sure you get a good nights sleep, you are going to need your strength for tomorrow, you will need to be able to ride a horse confidently by dusk tomorrow, it won't be easy, but I have every faith in you my friend" and she squeezed Fidelmas hand. Fidelma squeezed the fairys hand back and smiled. When they had finished drinking their tea Fairy Áine stood up "Alright Fidelma, let's go and get you home"

Chapter 11

Fidelma was back in her room, sitting on her bed, it was still light outside but she desperately wanted to go to sleep. She went downstairs and walked into the sitting room where her parents were watching T.V, "What's on?" She asked her Mother, sitting down beside her, "Oh the soaps, you know, the usual" she answered smiling at her daughter, Fidelma just smiled back and rested her head on her Mothers shoulder "Are you tired love?" her Mother asked "Mmmm" answered Fidelma "I'm wrecked" "Ah" said her Mother, "that'll be all the excitement from the party, why don't you go on up and have an early night for yourself?" Fidelma yawned "I think I will" Her Mother patted her knee, "Go on up love" she said "I'll bring you up a cup of tea"

Fidelma trudged up the stairs, she couldn't believe how tired she was, the soaps had started before she had her visit from Fairy Áine so she wasn't even gone that long in real time, it was going to be tough going between the two worlds, today was hard, how would she cope when the school holidays were over? She walked into her bedroom and began to change into her pyjamas; she smiled to herself as she imagined falling asleep at her desk in school. Maybe she would need to start taking some vitamins. She climbed into bed and let out a satisfied sigh, bed had never felt so good. So tomorrow she was going to learn to horse ride, she still couldn't believe it, she began to think of her Granny, she too had gone through all of this, how strange to imagine that now. Fidelma heard her Mothers footsteps on the stairs and she smiled, she came in with her lovely smile on her face as she carried the mug of tea over to the bed. Fidelma sat up and took the tea from her as her Mother sat down at the end of the bed "Are you ok luv?" she asked, Fidelma gave a watery smile "I'm fine Mam" she answered "I'm just really tired and you know how you get a bit emotional when you're tired" she smiled wryly. Mrs. Doyle patted her daughter's legs and smiled "Oh I know" she laughed "I know, get a good rest love, see you in the morning" and out she went, closing over the door behind her.

Fidelma sat in her bed with her knees pulled up under her blanket and her mug of tea resting on top of her knees, she was lost in thought again, here she was at home snuggled up nice and warm and cosy in her bed with a nice warm cup of tea, made and carried up the stairs to her by a Mother who loved her and would do anything for her, she thought of her Dad sitting down stairs, watching the soaps he pretends to hate, and her brother Sean who was at work but would no doubt be home soon, this was her home, this was her haven, she was safe here, she was loved and she was extremely lucky. Fidelma felt her eyes fill with tears as she thought about the Children of Lir and their lives in comparison with her own and she vowed to never complain again.

Chapter 12

Fidelma had her alarm set for 6am, she kept it under her pillow so as not to wake anyone else or her Mother would be wondering why her 16 year old daughter wanted to be up at 6am during the summer holidays. She blinked and stretched after turning off her alarm, she was so tired but knew she better get up and dressed before Fairy Áine came for her. She quickly pulled on her tracksuit and was just tying her laces when she noticed the treasure chest give a little rattle before the lid popped open and out bounced Fairy Áine, she flew straight over to Fidelma and kissed her on the tip of her nose "Good morning sleepy head" she smiled, Fidelma couldn't help but smile back at her little friend "Good morning" she replied before taking

Fairy Áines hand and starting her journey to the other world.

Once in An Crann darach Sean Fairy Áine pulled out a chair for Fidelma to sit on at the table, another fairy produced a mug of sweet tea and yet another fairy arrived with a steaming bowl of porridge. No sooner had both been placed before her and another fairy appeared with a small bowl which she placed on the table beside Fidelmas bowl of porridge, Fidelma peeked into it to see it filled to the brim with sticky golden syrup and a honey dipper sticking out of it. Fairy Áine came and sat down beside her as the other fairies set a place for her too "Made fresh this morning" smiled Fairy Áine, Fidelma looked up at her. Fairy Áine nodded at the small bowl "The honey, it was made fresh this morning, you'll love it!" Fidelma smiled "Oh yummy thank you, I love honey!" "I know" smiled Fairy Áine, "so did your Granny" and they both smiled at each other before tucking into the creamy porridge.

Fidelma enjoyed her breakfast but it was time to get to work. Fairy Áine stood up, "Ok" she began "We're going to go outside where your horse will be waiting, his name is Dílis, he's an absolute beauty, we chose well for you Fidelma" They walked out of An Crann darach Sean with two other fairies. Fidelma gasped at what she saw, standing in front of her were two stunningly beautiful creatures. One, a snow white horse, perfect from head to toe, like something from a picture book, the other a creature who, could be mistaken for a human woman, if it were not for the dear like antlers sprouting out from the top of her head. She had the most beautiful, thick, wavy auburn hair cascading down around her shoulders and down past her hips, her skin of alabaster was as white as the horse, but even with all these striking attributes, the one that caught Fidelmas attention most, were her enormous brown eyes, they were larger than the average human eye and even though her hair was a deep, shiny auburn, her thick eyebrows and extra-long eyelashes were jet black in contrast.

Fairy Áine spoke first "Fidelma, this is Flidais, Goddess of the woods and wild creatures" she gestured to the strange creature in front of them, Fidelma did not quite know how to greet this Flidais, she was still transfixed by her, should she shake her hand? Courtesy? She certainly looked like a Goddess in her forest green velvet dress. The beautiful creature simply bowed her head at the introduction so Fidelma just done the same in return. Fairy Áine then flew over to the horse and touched her tiny hand to his thick neck, "And this" she said "is the beautiful Dílis, his name means loyal, so Fidelma that is exactly what he will be, a forever companion that will be by your side throughout your time here" Fidelma walked slowly over to the beast, she too placed her hand on his thick neck, as soon as she did Dílis turned his big brown eyes towards her and stared for a moment, Fidelma smiled at him feeling like he was summing her up. "Ok" said Fairy Áine "I shall leave you to it" and away she fluttered back into An Crann darach Sean leaving Fidelma standing with Dílis and the stunning Flidais.

Flidais walked over to Dílis and began to smooth his face, she then took Fidelmas hand and gently placed it onto the horses muzzle, Dílis sniffed her hand "Hello Dílis" whispered Fidelma and the horse nuzzled it's head against her. "Good" smiled Flidais "he likes you, now let us get you up and on his back" Fidelma gulped, she could not believe what she was about to do, she felt like she should have written permission from her parents for something like this. Fidelma followed Flidais around to the side of Dílis where there was a log waiting for her to step onto, Flidais took Fidelmas hand again "Step up onto the log first" "Oh" said Fidelma "What about a saddle?" Flidais' face was that of puzzlement "What?" She simply asked. Fidelma thought for a moment, she looked around and spotted a basket behind where Flidais stood with what seemed to be a blanket and some apples and suddenly realised that there was a good chance there would be no saddle. "Em, it's just" she ventured "I was wondering do I just sit on his back? Or do I put something underneath me?" Flidais frowned at Fidelma as she considered her request, she said nothing but simply turned and fetched the blanket from the basket and draped it over the horses back while Fidelma stood on the log watching her. Flidais looked at Fidelma again with her enormous brown eyes, she took Fidelmas right hand and placed it across the front of the horses back, she then took her left hand and placed it on the rein closest to them "Hold on to this" she said "then you need to hoist yourself up using your left leg and throwing your right leg over as far as you can" Fidelma gulped, was she serious? Just like that? She was glad the log was about the height of Dílis knee otherwise she didn't think she would stand a chance. She gave a couple of little bounces and then hoisted herself up but came back down again, jeez this was harder than it sounded, and it did not sound easy. "Alright" said Flidais gently "deep breath and try again". After three attempts Fidelma was up on the back of Dílis, she smiled triumphantly down at Flidais "Well done" she said approvingly. Fidelma was thrilled with herself. Flidais walked around to the front of Dílis and spoke first to

Fidelma "Hold on tight to the reins, straighten your back, keep your legs long and your heels down" Fidelma did as she was told. Flidais then spoke to Dílis, kissing him on the nose before she spoke "Siúl" she said gently and Dílis took off ever so smoothly. Fidelma held onto the reins for dear life as the horse moved forward, she was thankful to notice that Flidais was walking along beside them.

Inside An Crann Darach Sean Fairy Áine was watching them from a little side window. Another fairy approached her "How is she doing?" Fairy Áine smiled at her "Foirfe, perfect! Just as I imagined, I think we are very lucky with Fidelma" Another Fairy approached "King Lír has sent word" Fairy Áine turned around to see the other fairy holding a scroll "Shall I go ahead and read it?" asked the fairy of her Queen. "Please" nodded Fairy Áine.

"My Dear Fairy Áine, Queen of Fairies" began the fairy before continuing "I hope my note finds you well, I however am not well, I fear I am developing a fever, apparently sleeping on the shore of the lake is bad for my health and I have been ordered to take to my bed, however I will only do this if I can have your word that you and your

Protector will indeed save my beautiful children, for that is the only outcome worth living for. While I am enduring my bed rest could I also ask that you send someone to watch over my beloved children, I cannot bear to think of them alone on the lake, especially at night" The young fairy looked at her Queen then back at the paper "It is simply signed then, Le gach deá ghui , King Lír."

There was silence for a moment while the two fairies waited for Fairy Áine to consider the note. "Alright" announced Fairy Áine clapping her hands "Call a meeting in the main room" The two fairies bowed and scurried off.

Moments later Fairy Áine entered the main room to a crowd of curious fairies and the hum of them quietly discussing with each other what this meeting might be about. Fairy Áine simply raised her right arm in the air and the room fell silent, she looked around her before speaking "Thank you all for gathering, I have had word from King Lír, I am afraid he is not well and has been ordered to take bed rest, this of course means that the children will be on their own on the lake and I am sure night time will be hardest for them. King Lír has asked that I send someone to watch over them, however this is what we will do" Fairy Áine looked around the room and chose four fairies, calling out their names "Fergus, Peadar, Gittan and Pirkko" The four fairies (two male and two female) approached their Queen "Fergus, you are a fairy with boundless energy" declared the Queen "Peadar, you are our rock, Gittan and Pirkko you are both powerful and strong and so I have chosen you four to go to Lake Derravaragh and on the shore build a sort of hut, a shelter where King Lír or whomever it is will be watching over the children, can have some warmth, a place to light a fire and shelter from the wind and rain, it does not need to be excessive in its size, I would however like it to be comfortable. You may go and start that now, go raibh maith agat, you are excused" and with that the four fairies bowed to their Queen and left the room.

Fairy Áine addressed the rest of the fairies "Berach, I would like you to draw up a roster for fairies staying on the shore of Lake Derravaragh for not only might the children be lonesome but I have not yet learnt what has become of the evil Aoife so the children could still be in danger" Berach nodded as Fairy Áine continued "so yes they will be there to keep them company but also to protect them should any danger arise, Viona and Casey you both can start tonight, the shelter should be somewhat ready by then, once Berach has the rota drawn up he will erect it here in the main room so you will all need to become familiar with it." The Queen paused for a moment before she continued "Fairy Caoimhe I would like you to prepare Eimhin for a journey, I shall go now and visit King Lír to outline our intentions to him, it will be late when I get back so when Fidelma returns, tell her where I am and make sure she is fed well for she will be hungry and tired after her day of training"

The meeting ended and the fairies all went about their business, Fairy Áine went to her room to change and prepare for her trip to see King Lír. She opened her wardrobe and took out a satchel and some travel clothes which she changed into, she then went to the kitchen to get a canteen of water and some berries to put in her satchel. Fairy Caoimhe came looking for her "Queen Áine, Eimhin is ready and waiting" Fairy Áine put her hand on

Fairy Caoimhes shoulder "Go raibh maith agat Caoimhe, I shall be back at dusk." And out she went.

Outside Fairy Áine climbed aboard the faithful Eimhin and headed off on her long journey. It was a lovely morning, the sun was up now and there wasn't a single cloud in the bright blue sky, she was enjoying the ride through the beautiful countryside, it was peaceful and it gave her time to think, she had so much on her mind at the moment, she knew there was always something happening in her world but she thought she would have had time to train Fidelma in first. Her thoughts were suddenly interrupted when Eimhin came to an abrupt halt. "Woah" soothed Fairy Áine "What is it boy? What's the matter?" Eimhin began sniffing the air before becoming startled and racing towards a hedge where he took shelter. Fairy Áine continued to soothe him, this was out of character for the hare so she knew something had scared him, animals were exceptional at sensing danger before the said danger could be seen, so as quietly as she could, Fairy Áine climbed down from Eimhins back, she tiptoed to the forefront of the hedge and peeked out from between some leaves, she couldn't see anything but they both stayed perfectly still, watching, listening, all she could hear was the sound of birds singing when all of a sudden she felt Eimhin tense beside her, a shadow cast over the land around the hedge, the birdsong had stopped and there was an eerie silence all around them, Fairy Áine kept her eyes looking out from the hedge as she silently reached her hand back and gently patted Eimhins head, he was trembling, something very frightening was outside and Fairy Áine did not like that she had no idea what it was. A couple of minutes passed and they heard a whooshing sound as the shadow disappeared, the birdsong returned and Eimhin stopped shaking.

Fairy Áine looked at him as he began to move out from under the hedge, clearly relieved, Fairy Áine followed him out; she looked around her but could not see anything out of the ordinary so she climbed back on Eimhin and they resumed their journey.

Eventually Fairy Áine arrived at King Lírs castle; once again the impressive building was shrouded by dark clouds and drizzle. One of King Lírs servants met Fairy Áine at the entrance, she was a small plump woman with a soft round face and kind eyes, today she looked distressed as she greeted the fairy "Oh Queen Fairy Áine" she said bowing "It is so good to see you, I am terribly worried about the King, I have made him some broth but cannot get him to take it, he needs to build up his strength for those children, they need him, he is all they have." Fairy Áine touched her tiny hand to the servant ladys face "I will speak with him Ardeen, take me to him" Ardeen nodded and made her way back to the entrance with Fairy Áine fluttering closely behind, they went up a dark staircase to a landing where there were 3 large rooms, Fairy Áine knew these to be the children's bedrooms and was sad to see the doors closed firmly on them in the darkness, they turned a corner and went up another dark staircase which led to the Kings room. Ardeen nodded nervously to Fairy Áine "It is alright" said the fairy "I can take it from here you just knock on the door and announce me then go and keep that broth warm, for the King will be needing some soon" and she smiled at the kind lady. Ardeen knocked at the big heavy door "King Lír, Fairy Áine Queen of fairies is here to see you" and she opened the door for the little fairy to go in while she returned to the kitchen.

Fairy Áine fluttered into the big room, the heavy curtains were drawn, the room was dark and extremely gloomy, she looked over to where King Lír was lying in his enormous bed and heard him let out a rumbly cough, she flew over to him and cleared her throat. "Ahem, King Lír I have come to meet with you as we have much to discuss, but how are you on this day?" The King turned over slowly in the bed, he looked at the fairy for a moment before responding scathingly "The little Queen who hails from Munster" Fairy Áine frowned, was he being rude to her? She could not be sure but she did know that his heart was broken and that a broken heart can make a person say things they would not usually say.

"I have come to personally assure you that we will indeed be helping you and your children" said the fairy but she was interrupted.

"And how exactly does the little Queen intend to do this?" shouted the King. Poor Fairy Áine jumped with fright, she gathered herself, she was standing on the small table beside the Kings bed "Excuse me King" she spoke loud and clear "you asked for my help and I have promised to do my utmost, I know you are suffering and we have been friends for many many years but I want you to remember that I have always been loyal to you and respected you and in return I expect the same" she lifted her little chin as she looked at him, King Lír was stunned for a moment but then he slowly pulled himself up in the bed to a sitting position, he took a sip of water from the cup at his bedside and cleared his throat.

"Forgive me Fairy Áine" begged the King "I have no right to take my anger and frustration out on you my friend, but if I am honest, I cannot see a way out of this horror"

Fairy Áine sat down on the table and looked at her old friend "I can tell you that at this very moment I have no idea how to solve this situation but we are working on it and I am confident that we will come up with a solution, but you need to be patient" The King nodded solemnly at the little fairy, she carried on "So far what I have decided to do for now is to set up a rota with my fairies for them to stay on the shore to watch over your children so they will never be on their own, as we speak 4 of my fairies are constructing a hut beside the lake for your shelter and comfort, we need you in good health" She jumped down onto the Kings bed, landing near his shoulder, she sat down and patted him with her tiny hand, the King gave her a watery smile "You are a good friend" he said. Fairy Áine simply smiled back "Have you spoken to Bodb Dearg?" she asked. King Lír's face darkened as he slammed his fist down on his bed making the tiny fairy jump "He is not welcome here!" he shouted. Fairy Áine patted him soothingly "Take it easy King Lír, you must mind your health" The King reached over and took another drink from his water. Fairy Áine waited a moment until he seemed calmer before she spoke again "You must not take your anger out on him either, he is your family, he had no hand in this and in your heart you know that! Bodb loves those children as much as you do and they love him in return, you need to stay united for their sake"

King Lír shook his head as his eyes filled with tears, this time when he spoke it were much quieter as his voice was full of emotion "He is her father! It is because of him that I married that wretched creature"

"That is true" replied Fairy Áine, "but remember, he was also the Father of Aoibh, you loved her with all your heart, she was a kind and gentle creature who bore you your four beautiful children" The King began to weep much to the fairy's distress, she continued carefully "I know you are hurting, but you must be strong for the sake of the children, they will need your strength to help them through this. We are giving Fidelma some training at the minute and then I will take her with me to pay a visit to Bodb Dearg, we need to find out as much as we can about Aoife, what drove her to do such an unimaginable act and where she is now, we will not solve this until then" Fairy Áine stood up "The servant who you mentioned was asked by Aoife to end the childrens lives" The King looked at Fairy Áine "Where is he now?" she asked.

"Aengus, he is at his home" replied the King "I was very grateful to him for his loyalty to me and to the children, but he was badly shaken, speak with Ardeen on your way out, she will tell you which house is his" Fairy Áine bowed and flew towards the door before stopping "I will be in touch soon, now make sure you eat what Ardeen has prepared for you" King Lír simply nodded.

Fairy Áine was outside the castle grounds, making her way towards the home of the servant Aengus, she was glad the late afternoon sun still had some heat in it as herself and Eimhin followed the directions given by the kind Ardeen, eventually they came to a small humble dwelling. Fairy Áine took some berries out of her satchel and put them on the ground for Eimhin "here ye go boy, I won't be long" and she went and knocked on the front door. She waited for a moment before the door was opened by a small wiry woman with a pointed face "Hello?" she asked when she seen the little fairy fluttering at the door, Fairy Áine spoke clearly "Hello, I am Fariy Áine, Queen of fairies, I am a good friend of King Lír and was wondering if I could speak with Aengus?" The woman seemed to hesitate for a moment before standing back and inviting the little fairy into her house. Inside the house was small but tidy, there were 3 small children playing on the floor and in the corner of the room sitting on a small stool staring into the fire was a man whom Fairy Áine presumed was Aengus. He did not seem to notice her come in; the woman spoke first "Aengus, Aengus! You have a visitor" Aengus looked up slowly and eyed the fairy "I know you" he said quietly "You are the fairy Queen"

"Yes" The fairy made her way closer to the man "My name is Fairy Áine and I was wondering if I could speak with you?" The man simply nodded and gestured to a small seat beside him; Fairy Áine flew down and sat on the edge of the seat. The woman busied herself with a pot of water and the children continued to play. "King Lír tells me that Aoife asked you to . ." Aengus jumped up from his seat interrupting the fairy "She asked me to do the unthinkable, that wicked woman! I hope I never lay eyes on her again"

The children had stopped their game and were staring up at their father, the youngest one started to cry, Aengus scooped him up and nursed him on his knee, he wiped at his eyes before he spoke again "I have children of my own" Fairy Áine could feel his distress "I know" she spoke calmly "What she asked of you *was* unthinkable and King Lír is grateful to you but I just need you to tell me what happened if you do not mind and then I will leave you be." Aengus nodded, his wife approached with a steaming mug of tea for her husband and a thimble of tea for their guest. "I have worked for the King since I was a boy" said

Aengus as his young son climbed down from his lap to continue his game with his siblings "It used to be such a happy place, when King Lír married Aoibh you could feel the love they held for each other and when each child was born that love just grew, but when Aoibh was taken from them the sadness was almost unbearable, if it were not for the children I do not know what would have become of the King, but the children made him happy and slowly the castle became a happy place again, that is until Aoife came to live there. She made the children uncomfortable, we all knew that but not one of us said it to the King" he shook his head sadly and wiped at his eyes again "he is a good King but we are but his servants, it would not have been our place to speak to him of such things" He looked at Fairy Áine pleadingly "Of course" she agreed "I understand, go on"

Aengus took a mouthful of tea and then continued "As I said, when she came to live at the castle, things changed, she did not speak nice to us, the servants, not the way King Lír did, or indeed the way Aoife used to, but it was the children we were worried about, they became distant and King Lír seemed to be spending so much time with his new wife. Then one day she came to me, she said . . . . she said she feared the children were of evil heart. . . I told her that was madness but she was insistent, she grabbed my wrist and said that I must take them into the forest and end their lives" once again Aengus wiped at his eyes and took a long mouthful from his tea, he continued, shaking his head as though reliving the conversation "I told her no, I told her I would never do such a thing and the King would have her head, then she told me that I had given her the correct answer, I said I did not understand and she said that it was a test and that I had passed for she could never hurt the children. I turned to leave but she stopped me then and said that if I breathed a word of this to the King then she would turn my beautiful children into wild boars, I told her *she* was of wicked heart but she just became hysterical and said that she was not wicked but if I were to tell any of it to the King she would have no choice but to take action" Aengus began to weep "I was frightened for my own children, I did not know what to do, I could not sleep that night and the next morning when I went to the castle she looked at me and her green eyes seemed to glow and I knew then that I would not tell, however that evening when we heard about the children of King Lír, I told my wife this story and she told me I must go at once and tell the King, and so I did".

Fairy Áine had listened intently to the story "Did she speak to you the next day? To any of you?" Aengus shook his head "No" he said "She just announced she was taking the children to visit their Grandfather and would return the following day, I was happy because I knew they would be safe with Bodb Dearg. I had no idea they would not make it there." Fairy Áine shook her head sadly, "Poor Bodh Dearg he must be feeling heartbroken too" she muttered her despair half to herself half to Aengus.

"Oh he is" said Aengus "he too looks like a broken man" Fairy Áine looked up "What?" she said "you have seen him?"

"Bodb Dearg?" asked Aengus "Of course, he has come to the castle every day since but King Lír sends him away each time"

"Oh" sighed Fairy Áine "This is not good, not good at all" She stood up and handed her now empty thimble to

Aengus "Thank you for telling me your story Aengus, please know that nothing you could have done would have changed things" Aengus just gave a weak smile as a reply, Fairy Áine turned to his wife "Thank you for making me welcome in your home" The woman smiled at the little fairy and said "Please, bring back the children" Fairy Áine nodded, she knew she could make no promises. She left the house and climbed up on Eimhins back again as they headed on their journey back to An Crann darach Sean.

It was dusk when they arrived back at the old oak tree, Fairy Áine was very happy to see it as Eimhin came up over the hill, she climbed down and patted him on the head "Thank you Eimhin" The hare sniffed at her hand "yes yes" giggled the fairy and she reached into her satchel for some more berries which she scattered on the ground for her swift companion "I think you have earned them" she smiled and made her way into an Crann darach Sean.

As always it was a hive of activity and sitting at the table in the midst of it all was Fidelma tucking into a bowl of stew. Fairy Áine smiled, hung up her satchel and made her way over to the table, she sat down beside

Fidelma "So" she said "How was it?" Fidelma dropped her spoon and threw her arms around the fairy "Oh Fairy Áine you're back, I'm so glad to see you, I had such a wonderful day, I just love Dílis, he's amazing and I rode him through the field all by myself" Fairy Áine laughed at Fidelma, she'd never seen anyone so animated, it was so refreshing after the day she had had. "Oh Fidelma" she smiled at her friend "You are very welcome, I knew you and Dílis would be a good match, how is the stew?" "Oh yum" claimed Fidelma, tucking into the food again "It's just delicious, it tastes just like the stew my Granny used to make" Fairy Áine smiled "It would do, she seen us make it enough times" she called to one of the fairy's "Fairy Caoimhe? Could I have mine now please?" Fairy Caoimhe was in the kitchen "Of course, I shall bring it now" and a moment later she sat a steaming bowl of stew and a basket of bread in front of her Queen.

Fairy Áine took a few spoonfuls of her food before addressing Fidelma again "Fidelma" she began "Tomorrow is going to be another busy day I am afraid, you are going to have some archery lessons in the morning and then meet with Cailte Mac Ronain in the afternoon, the day after that we will go and see Bodb Dearg, I do not want to put it off any longer"

Fidelma nodded in between spoonfuls, she picked up some bread and tore a piece off "Can I ask, who is Cailte Mac Ronain?"

Fairy Áine smiled "You will like him Fidelma, he is a fascinating man, he can run as fast as any great horse, he tells the most amazing stories but most importantly for you, he can communicate with animals"

Fidelma stopped what she was doing and stared in astonishment at the fairy

"Say that again? He can communicate with animals?" she asked. "Yes" said Fairy Áine "He can both speak *to* them and understand what they are saying, it is a practise you will need, you have no idea what a help it will be to you here and won't it be nice for you to be able to communicate with Dílis?" Fidelma was still looking at her friend bewildered "T t talk to animals?" she stammered. "Yes" giggled fairy Áine "You will spend the morning with him and over the next few weeks you will meet for more lessons, he has very kindly agreed to teach you, you should be honoured for he is highly thought of."

Fidelma just looked dumfounded; she was unsure how to reply so she didn't. Fairy Áine continued eating her food, after a moment she spoke again "Fidelma I have had a heart wrenching day as I am sure you can imagine, King Lír is in an awful state, I just hope we can help him" The fairy's eyes filled with tears as she was lost in thought for a moment, Fidelma put her hand over Fairy Áines hand "We will" she said comfortingly "We will find a way."

Chapter 13

Fidelma was back in her bedroom, she looked at the clock beside her bed, it was 6:35, she shook her head, she felt like a time traveller, it was so strange. She sat on her bed and smiled as she thought about the lovely Dílis, she loved him, what a pity her friends could not see him. She wondered what the archery lessons would be like, would she be any good? She had no idea and Cailte Mac Ronain, what would he be like? Talk to animals? She could not get her head around it. Then her thoughts travelled to the children of Lír, would all of this training mean she would be able to help them? Would they be free again? What if she could not help them? Fidelma shook her head, it was all a bit much for her, one thing she did know for sure though as she pulled off her runners and stripped out of her tracksuit, was that she was getting into bed and sleeping till lunch time, she got into her pyjamas, climbed into bed and was asleep moments later.

*****

Fidelma was woken by a tapping sound, she rubbed at her eyes and looked at her clock, it read 12:40, she looked around the room, the tapping sound was coming from the window, she climbed out of bed and walked over to open the curtains. Fidelma jumped when she pulled the curtain back to see a huge black crow sitting on the outside window sill, banging its beak at the glass, it stopped suddenly, it too seemed startled, they stared at each other for a moment before the crow start cawing loudly and pecking at the window again, Fidelma banged at the window "Go away you ugly bird" and the bird took off, she smiled at herself, maybe tomorrow she would understand a crow.

Fidelma slipped her feet into her slippers and made her way downstairs, she went straight into the kitchen where her Mother was making her way through a basket of ironing. "Ooh" smiled her Mother "Good afternoon lazy bones" Fidelma gave a big stretch and yawn "Aww heya Mam, I needed that sleep I was so tired" Mrs. Doyle continued ironing "Well stick the kettle on luv and I'll make us a nice cup of tea, I'm almost done here, I've the house cleaned from top to bottom and a basket of ironing done before you've even started your day" Fidelma smiled to herself as she filled the kettle with water, if only her Mother knew what she herself had been up to, she sat the kettle on its base, flicked the switch and got two cups down from the cupboard.

"Any plans for today?" asked Mrs Doyle. Fidelma pulled a stool out from the counter and sat down "Not really" she said "I was going to go to the library later maybe." Mrs Doyle stopped mid fold of a t-shirt "The library?" she asked "Sure you're still on your school holidays, what's taking ye to the library?" Fidelma shrugged "I dunno, just some stuff I want to look up, sure won't it get me out of the house" Mrs. Doyle plugged out the iron "Well fair play to ye so", the kettle boiled and she walked over to make the tea.

Mrs. Doyle made two cups of tea and brought them to the counter where Fidelma was sitting; she placed one in front of her daughter and sat down beside her with her own cup. "Thanks Mam" said Fidelma "Mam, did you ever do horse riding when you were younger?" Mrs. Doyle swallowed a mouthful of tea "Horse-riding?" she asked taken aback "God no, don't think there was ever the opportunity growing up in Dublin, mind you, I think your Granny did, I've a vague memory of her talking fondly of a horse, not sure though" Fidelma just smiled, of course her Granny did. Mrs. Doyle was intrigued "Why are ye asking about horse riding? You're not looking for a horse are ye? Don't think our back garden is big enough" she said laughing. "No no" said Fidelma "no I was just asking, I had a dream I was horse riding and was just thinking about it that's all" "Well" said Mrs. Doyle "You may dream about getting up a bit earlier tomorrow so we can head into town and pick you up some stuff for school before the shops run out." Fidelma just nodded and smiled.

After Fidelma had her cup of tea and some toast she went for a shower and got changed to head out to the library. They were lucky; they had a library not too far from them so she could walk to it. Fidelma loved the library, she always did since she was a little girl, she loved the smell of books and the calmness of the library. She walked in through the door and the girl at the counter smiled at her, Fidelma smiled back "Hi" and she made her way down to the 'Irish Interest' section. Fidelma wasn't too sure what she was looking for, she looked at books that were for people learning the Irish language, she was pretty good at Irish in school, would she need to get books to learn more? She didn't think so. She wandered on through the aisle until she came to a section on Irish Mythology; she walked along looking intently at the books on the shelves, so many books, some with dust on them. What was she looking for? Fidelma wasn't too sure but she desperately wanted to help the Children of Lír so they didn't end up spending 900 years as swans, it was unbearable to think about it. She pulled out 5 books and brought them over to a table, she opened her backpack and produced a pen and a writing pad. Fidelma spent two hours in the library, scouring through the books for clues. Most people in Ireland had heard of the story of the Children of Lír, but the story always went that the spell could only be broken when the children heard the ringing of a Christian bell, why then was that not the case? She had no idea, it was all so confusing. She looked through her scribbled notes,

    Tuatha De Danann,   Swans —
    shape shifters

    Lake Derravaragh   Knockeyon

Straits of Moyle

Isle of Inis Glora

900 years!!!

King Lír - Ruler of the Sea!! Fomorians!!

Fidelma sat looking at her notes, not a lot for 2 hours research she thought tapping her pen off the table, does any of it mean anything? She had no idea but she would take them home and read more into them on the internet, see if that would give her any hints.

Fidelma packed up her backpack, put three of the books back on the shelf and took the other two up to the counter to check them out, then she popped them in her bag and made her way home. It was late in the afternoon, a nice dry bright day and she was enjoying the short walk, she turned the corner of her street and on the footpath in front of her stood a big black crow, stopping Fidelma in her tracks. "Jesus ye scared me" she muttered putting her hand to her chest, the bird seemed to be staring at her menacingly, its feathers were raised which just made it look evil to Fidelma but then she shook her head "You're a crow!" she muttered "what am I like?" and she went to walk on but as soon as she did the Crow extended its large wings, bent its head and took flight, Fidelma quickly realised it was heading straight for her head, she ducked just in time as it flew directly over her, its vast crows feet barely missing the top of her head, she could not believe it! Fidelma turned around to see where it went, it landed on the footpath behind her, slowly it turned around and stared at her again, its feathers began to raise and Fidelma was not going to wait for it to attack again so she ran, she covered her head with her hands as she ran and sure enough the crow came at her again, this time catching her hands with its sharp claws, Fidelma let out a yelp as she got to her driveway and ran up to the doorway while rooting in her pocket for her key, as she was putting her key in the door, hands shaking, she could hear the crow cawing loudly, she got the door open, ran in and shut it behind her with a loud bang, she leaned against it for a moment panting. Mrs. Doyle came out from the kitchen "What's going on Fidelma?" Fidelma looked up at her and looked at her bloodied hands, her Mother rushed to her "Jesus Mary and Joseph what happened to ye? Did ye fall?" She put her arm around her daughter and guided her into the kitchen. "Jesus love you're shaking, here sit down" She sat Fidelma down on a stool at the counter and took her hands in her own hands "Mother of God look at your hands" she touched Fidelmas face "What happened to ye?" Fidelma was still shaking, the tears were running down her face but she felt stupid, what had happened? She got attacked by a crow? Seriously? "I was attacked" she muttered, her Mother gasped "What? By who?" Fidelma closed her eyes "By a crow" she said quietly. Mrs Doyle looked at her daughter like she was going mad "What?" she asked "A crow? A bird like?" Fidelma opened her eyes and gave a watery smile "Yes Mam, I know it sounds mad but there was this big crow and it just came at me, I dunno maybe its nesting season or something I dunno" Mrs. Doyle kept looking at her "A crow?" she asked her daughter again. Fidelma nodded, her Mother lifted up her hands for Fidelma to see "So you're telling me a crow did this to ye?" Fidelma looked at her hands now, they were all cut and bloody "Yes Mam" she said "I put my hands over my head to protect it" Mrs. Doyle stared at her for a moment then she shook her head "Mother of God, I don't know, I've never heard the likes" She walked over to the sink and turned on the tap, produced a small basin from the cupboard under the sink and a bottle of Savlon, she poured a small drop into the basin and then added the water, giving it a swirl with her hand. "Ah no Mam" pleaded Fidelma "Not the Savlon" Her Mother just nodded "Ye have to Fidelma, you need to give those cuts a good clean, God knows what you could catch off them dirty crows" she put the basin on the counter in front of Fidelma and eased Fidelmas hands down into it "Ahhhhhhh" groaned her daughter as the Savlon began to sting, Mrs. Doyle patted her arm "I know love, but that just means it's working, sit like that for a minute and I'll make ye a nice cup of sweet tea for the shock."

Mrs. Doyle made two mugs of tea, she placed one in front of Fidelma, she then got a hand towel and walked around to where her daughter was sitting, she held the towel out on her hands "here, give me your hands" she said, Fidelma lifted her hands out of the water and rested them on the towel, Mrs. Doyle began to gently pat them dry "Now" she said "there ye are, have some tea" She took the basin away, emptied it down the sink and hung the towel back on its little hook, she then left the kitchen and reappeared a moment later with the Medicine Box which she sat on the counter. Mrs. Doyle pulled out a stool beside her daughter and began rooting in the box, taking out bits and pieces. "We'll get them hands patched up luv" she said as she busied herself cutting up bandages. Fidelma smiled fondly at her Mother "Thanks Mam".

Once her hands were bandaged up, Fidelma made her way upstairs to her bedroom and sat down on her bed, she looked at her hands and shook her head "What the heck?" she muttered to herself "Crazy crow" She got up to get her laptop, looking out the window she stared for a moment, sitting high in the tree in her front garden was a large black crow, it seemed to be looking in at her. Fidelma took a step back from the window, still looking out, is it possible that it was the same crow that attacked her? The same crow that was on her window ledge that morning? Why though? What had she ever done on the crow? She shook her head, she had no idea, she gathered up her laptop and sat back down on her bed with it on her lap, powering it up, her backpack was on her bed beside her; she grabbed her notebook from it and opened it up on her notes.

****

Later that evening, Fidelma was lying on her bed having a rest listening to some music when she heard her Mother calling her from downstairs. Fidelma walked to the top of the stairs and shouted down "Yes Mam?" Mrs. Doyle shouted back up "Come down for a minute love, your Dad wants to talk to ye" Fidelma shrugged and walked down the stairs into the sitting room where her Dad was sitting in his usual spot, her Mam was standing at the door "Your Dad just wants to talk to ye for a minute love, sit down" Fidelma frowned slightly, this seemed a bit weird and somewhat awkward, she had the feeling that something was wrong. Mr. Doyle pressed the mute button on the remote control and leaned forward in his chair, resting his arms on his knees "Howaya love" Fidelma looked at him puzzled "Eh heya Dad" Mr. Doyle shifted uncomfortably in his chair before he continued "your Mammy tells me ye had a bit of an accident" and he gestured towards her bandaged hands. Fidelma looked down at her injured hands and back at her Dad "Yeah" Mr Doyle looked up at Mrs. Doyle and cleared his throat before speaking again "It's just that, your Mammy tells me you said you were attacked by

. . . . a crow" Fidelma looked from one to the other "Eh yeah, because I was" There was an awkward silence as her Mother and Father exchanged looks, Mrs Doyle came over to the couch and sat down beside her daughter putting her arm around her "It's ok love" she says "you're not in any trouble" Fidelma was dumbfounded she actually did not know what to say, she opened her mouth to speak but nothing came out. Her Father spoke again "We've noticed Aaron hasn't been around in a while, have you two fallen out?" Fidelma looked at them both, horrified "What? No! Of course not! Aaron is down with his cousin in Cork for the week, what are yis trying to say?" Her Mother answered first "We're not trying to say anything Fidelma" she looked at her husband who continues for her "No love we're just concerned, something's happened to you and we're worried that you don't feel you can tell us" Fidelma could not believe what she was hearing, she jumped up off the couch raising her voice slightly "Seriously, it was a crow, why would I lie"? Mr Doyle stood up and gently took his daughters hands in his own. "Fidelma" he said "you're telling us a crow did this to you? Really?" Fidelma shook her head and laughed "Yes Dad, I know it sounds ridiculous, it's so ridiculous you couldn't make it up" she walked towards the sitting room door taking her Dad gently by the arm "Come here, look" Fidelma made her way on out to the hallway and opened the front door, she stepped out onto the front step with her Dad, her Mother closely behind. "Look" said Fidelma pointing at the crow still sitting in the tree. The crow began cawing loudly "That's it, I'm pretty sure that's the same crow that attacked me, it's mad, and look at the size of him!" Mr. Doyle stepped down off the step and walked a bit closer to the tree, Fidelma stayed on the step with her Mother. The large crow looked menacingly at Mr. Doyle, bending its head it cawed loudly as its feathers cocked up "Dad!" shouted Fidelma "be careful, he looks like he's going to attack" No sooner had Fidelma shouted her warning than the bird took to flight, Mr. Doyle ducking just in time as it glided over his head, Mrs. Doyle pushed Fidelma back in behind the front door as the bird came towards them, she managed to get herself behind the door just in time as the crow banged loudly against it and droped onto the step. Mr. Doyle shouted into them "Stay in there, I'll sort it!" He made his way towards the bird just as it start to make its way shakily to its feet again, it hopped down off the step, stopped and looked at Fidelmas Father who was crouching down coming towards it with his hands out as if to try and catch the bird but the crow swiftly took to flight and was away before he even got a chance.

Mr. Doyle stood for a moment watching the big bird fly away before going back into the house, Mother and daughter are sitting on the end of the stairs, he smiled at them "Well?" asks his wife, Mr. Doyle just shrugged "It's gone" he said shaking his head "Doubt it'll be back, it gave itself a right knock on the head there" Fidelma and her Mam stood up and her Dad put his arms around her "I'm sorry love, we shouldn't have doubted ye, it was just a very strange story" Mrs. Doyle ruffled the top of Fidelmas head "I'm sorry too love, we were just worried, that's all, I've never in my life seen a crow like that, have you Sean?" Fidelmas Dad shook his head "Never." Fidelma smiled "It's ok" she said, relieved "I know it was unbelievable, but I promise you if there were anything wrong I would come to you both"

They walked into the kitchen where Mrs. Doyle put the kettle on; Fidelma sat at the counter with her Dad while her Mother busied herself getting cups and tea bags out. "Why don't we do something this Saturday?" asked Mr. Doyle all of a sudden, they both looked at him in surprise "Oh that'd be nice while the weather is still good" said Mrs. Doyle "What ye think Fidelma, what would ye like to do?" Fidelma looked from her Mother to her Father "Well" she started "there's a place in West Meath is supposed to be lovely, there's a big lake, Lake Derravaragh I think it's called, it's supposed to be beautiful, could we go there maybe?" Mrs. Doyle looked at her husband raising her eyebrows questioningly, he nodded his head "Yeah that sounds good, I went there years ago when I was a boy, my Father took us fishing, it's a nice spot alright, sure we'll do that so" he looked at Fidelma teasingly "You'll have to get up early though" Fidelma smiled "Yes I know, I am capable of getting up before noon you know" her parents laughed.

Later that evening as the sun was beginning to set Fidelma slipped away to her bedroom, she closed down her laptop and put it away, peering out the window as she did so, 'no sign of the crazy crow thank God' she thought to herself pulling the curtains and turning on her bedside lamp, no sooner done and Fairy Áine appeared, fluttering up and giving her usual greeting, a fairy kiss on Fidelmas forehead "Hello my dear friend" Fidelma smiled back "hi" but before she could say anything else Fairy Áine noticed her bandaged hands and gasped "Oh Fidelma, my goodness" her tiny hands flying to her mouth "What happened?" Fidelma just shook her head "Fairy Áine you wouldn't believe me even if I told you, but don't worry it looks worse than it is, I'm grand" and she took the fairy's hand, ready to be whisked away.

Chapter 14

Fidelma was sitting in An Crann darach Sean sipping tea beside a window, watching the sun rise over the hill outside, she was completely mesmerized by the beauty of it. Fairy Áine came over towards her "Fidelma, you have your Archery lessons this morning, do you think you will be able to manage it with your hands?" Fidelma looked at her bandaged hands "Ah yeah" she said "I'll be grand I'd say, they're just surface wounds." Fairy Áine nodded and took a seat on the little bench beside her friend at the window with her own mug of tea. "So, Fairy Eimear will be training you this morning" she said "she's a fairy of many talents, once she is finished with your archery lesson she will measure you for some clothes" Fidelma looked at her fairy friend in surprise "Clothes?" Fairy Áine nodded "yes Fidelma, I am sure your attire fits in well when you are at home but it is just not suitable for your time here, so Fairy Eimear will be making you some outfits. We have a room for you here which I will take you to see after we have our tea and your clothes, tools, instruments, weapons, whatever you use here will be stored there." Fidelma smiled nodding and took a sip of her tea, wondering vaguely what the new clothes would be like.

It was time for her Archery lesson. Fairy Eimear was a delicate looking fairy with a mop of curls on top of her head, "Follow me" she said and they both set off up over the hill. They stopped when they came to a large tree, carved into its trunk was a vast circle containing four smaller circles. Sitting on the ground beside the trunk were a bow and a small slim bag containing arrows. Fairy Eimear flew to within 10 metres from the tree. "Fidelma" she called pointing back to the tree "Over at the trunk is your bow and Quiver of arrows, bring them over here please" Fidelma did as she was asked, she picked up the bow and ran her hand along the wood of it, before picking up the bag which was full of arrows, it was made of a tough coarse brown material and had her name stitched into it in black thread, she made her way towards the fairy "It's got my name on it!" she exclaimed "Yes" smiled Fairy Eimear "I made it especially, it is full of arrows and it can be re stocked as you need, the bow I made myself too, it is good and strong. Now come stand beside me" Fidelma stood beside the fairy and waited further instruction "Now" spoke Fairy Eimear "Take an arrow from your quiver, turn and face the tree, point your feet toward the tree and place them shoulder width apart" She flew in front of Fidelma and inspected her stance "Hold the bow with your left hand, now point the bow towards the ground and place the shaft of the arrow on the arrow rest" she fluttered at the bow and pointed to the arrow rest "This here" she said helpfully, she then patted her tiny hand on three of Fidelmas fingers "use these three fingers to lightly hold the arrow on the string, now hold the bow arm outwards towards the target on the tree"

Back at An Crann darach Sean Fairy Áine was sitting at her table writing when fairy Caoimhe came into the room "Pardon me Fairy Áine but Cailte Mac Ronain is here." Fairy Áine looked up surprised "Oh" she said "He is early, send him in please Fairy Caoimhe" she put down her quill and packed away the paper she had been writing on. The door to the room opened and in walked a young man dressed in coarse trousers and heavy boots, he wore no clothes on the top half of his body apart from two bronze bracelet like rings on both upper arms, he had been made fairy size to allow him to enter An Crann Darach Sean but still he was an imposing figure in the room.

Cailte Mac Ronain opened his muscular arms out to the Fairy Queen as he walked into the room "Queen Fairy Áine" he exclaimed in his booming voice, Fairy Áine smiled affectionately at him and walked into his embrace. "Dia Dhuit Cailte" she greeted him fondly "It is so good to see you again, thank you for coming." The two friends took seats at the table as Fairy Caoimhe came in with a mug of tea for Cailte Mac Ronain "Go raibh maith agat Fairy Caoimhe" he boomed. He slurped a mouthful of tea before speaking "So, you have yourself a new recruit?" "We have" smiled Fairy Áine "and although she is very sweet, already I can tell she has strength like her Grandmother" Cailte nodded at the fairy "Good, good, well I will go over the basics with her today and then we can continue to work together, she has a horse I presume?" Fairy Áine nodded in reply "She does, his name is Dilís and he is foirfe, absolutely perfect, would you like to meet him while Fidelma is doing her archery?" Cailte continued nodding "Good good, yes I should meet with him first please, but not before I finish this tae" he slurped another mouthful "Ahhhh it is good, so I take it you two are going to see Bodb Dearg?" he asked of Fairy Áine "Yes" said Fairy Áine "I think we should go as soon as possible, we need to learn as much as we can about the wicked Aoife and what has become of her." Cailte Mac Ronain frowned as he shook his head "Hmmmmm" his voice rumbled "Uafásach! This business with the children of Lír is just uafásach" he looked up at Fairy

Áine who was sipping from her tea when he suddenly grasped her hand across the table "You *will* be careful Fairy Áine won't you?" Fairy Áine was slightly taken back by this sudden show of affection, she blinked a couple of times before replying "Of course *we* will be careful" she gently pulled her hand back and stood up from the table "I am always careful, I am perfectly capable of taking care of myself and my fairies, as is Fidelma" Cailte Mac Ronain stood up now too "I was not trying to suggest otherwise, but you are dealing with the Thuatha de Danann here, it could get dangerous, and, well" Cailte hesitated for moment as he seemed to be looking at something on his boots "you know I care for you and, well, just mind yourself is all" The pair stared at each other for a moment before Fairy Áine broke the silence "I will get Fairy Caoimhe to take you to Dilís" Cailte simply bowed his head to which Fairy Áine done the same in return before leaving the room.

Cailte Mac Ronain sat back down in his seat and sighed; he picked up his mug and continued to slurp at his tea, after a moment Fairy Caoimhe came back into the room. "Cailte" she announced smiling politely "Come with me, I shall take you to Dilís" Cailte Mac Ronain followed Fairy Caoimhe to the door where she took his hand and brought him outside the Oak Tree in the fairies usual way. Once outside they made their way companionably towards a field behind the Oak Tree where the impressive white horse stood grazing. As Cailte walked towards the horse, the little fairy fluttering along beside him, he spoke to her "So will you be making the trip to Bodb Deargs with Fairy Áine and Fidelma?" The fairy shook her little head "No, it will be just the two of them" she shot a look at the man striding along beside her "Do not worry Cailte, she can handle herself" Cailte looked at the fairy, she smiled at him and he smiled back.

Fairy Caoimhe stopped just before they came to Dilís and let Cailte carry on, she fluttered down to a wild mushroom and perched herself on it, watching as he approached the white beast. The horse heard the footsteps and looked up in the direction of Cailte, immediately Cailte put his arms out in front of him, his fingertips touching, his hands at an angle making the shape of an upside down V, the horse immediately bowed its head, it stayed like that until Cailte reached him,

Cailte put his hands gently on either side of the horses face, Dilís lifted his head up and the two made eye contact for a moment or two before Dilís began licking Cailtes hands and then his face. Cailte let out a big booming laugh "There ye go my friend, good boy, good boy." He looked back to Fairy Caoimhe sitting on the mushroom; she shook her head smiling and took off back to the Oak Tree.

Fairy Caoimhe entered the room where only a short time ago Cailte Mac Ronain had been sitting with Fairy Áine, this time Fairy Áine was sitting on her own at the table continuing with her writing. She looked up when she heard Fairy Caoimhe come in "Everything okay?" she asked, Fairy Caoimhe sat down across from her Queen and her friend "Yes, everything is okay, he has such a way with Dilís, it was fascinating to watch." "He has a way with all animals" was Fairy Áines simple and curt reply as she continued writing. Fairy Caoimhe watched her for a moment before speaking again "He was voicing his concerns about you going to see Bodh Dearg" Fairy Áine replied this time without looking up "Yes he voiced his concerns with me too but like I told him, I can look after myself" Fairy Caoimhe chewed on her bottom lip nervously "I think the fact that he is concerned should be noted" Fairy Áine gently put her quill down and closed her hands in front of her "Fairy Caoimhe, if you have something to say to me, say it, if not, a cup of tea would be much appreciated" The two fairies held eye contact for a moment until Fairy Caoimhe stood up from her seat "I will go make the tea" she said "Good" replied Fairy Áine as she picked up her quill and continued with her writing.

When Fairy Caoimhe came back in with the tea, Fairy Áine was standing by the window looking out, she walked over and handed her Queen a mug of tea and kept one for herself, she looked out the window to see Fidelma pull back her bow and launch an arrow, it landed right in the middle of the target on the tree, she looked at Fairy Áine who was smiling "She is doing good" said Fairy Áine "She is doing really good, she is going to make a good protector" "Yes" said Fairy Caoimhe "I think she will, she certainly has a good aim. Do you think she is ready for this trip though? So soon?" Fairy Áine turned and looked at her friend "Fairy Caoimhe, we really need to act on this, as it is we have already let too much time pass,

Fidelma will be ready, we will be fine, please, try not to worry" Fairy Áine smiled at her friend, Fairy Caoimhe nodded "I shall try" she replied. With that the door opened and Cailte Mac Ronain walked into the room "Well Dilís is a fine beast, you chose well" Fairy Caoimhe looked from one to the other "I shall leave you both to it" and she left the room. Fairy Áine replied then "Yes he is a beautiful horse, he was recommended to me by Flidais" "Yes" smiled Cailte "Dilís told me, he also told me that he quite likes Fidelma, he will indeed live up to his name and be very loyal to her" Fairy Áine smiled "That is good to hear thank you" The door opened and Fairy Caoimhe came back in "Excuse me Fairy Áine but Fidelma is finishing up, I am going to serve her up some lunch will you both be joining her?" Fairy Áine looked over at Cailte Mac Ronain questioningly to which he nodded "Yes Fairy Caoimhe" answered Fairy Áine then "we will both join her go raibh maith agat" Fairy Caoimhe simply nodded and left the room again. "We will have some food and then you can spend the afternoon with Fidelma" said Fairy Áine "Please try to fit in as much as you can today, tomorrow we head for Bodb Deargs"

Chapter 15

Fidelma was ravenous. She sat down at the long table and tried to control her growling tummy but the delicious hearty smell creeping up her nostrils was not helping matters. Suddenly the door opened and Fairy Áine walked in, followed by a very handsome young man who, much to Fidelmas surprise was naked from the waist up. They approached the table and Fairy Áine spoke "Fidelma, this is Cailte Mac Ronain, he is going to help you with conversing with animals." She turned to the man now standing beside her

"Cailte, this is Fidelma, our new protector." Cailte Mac Ronain walked around to where Fidelma was sitting and extended his hand "I have heard good things about you Fidelma". Fidelma stood up and took his hand, gulping and blinking as he shook it with vigour, she could not think of anyting to say to him, she was not used to shaking hands with handsome bare chested men so she just managed to mutter "ahem, yes, hello eh, thank you" she looked over at Fairy Áine who smiled and shook her head as she sat down opposite Fidelma, Cailte walked back around and took a seat beside her.

A petite red haired fairy with a face full of freckles approached with two baskets of fresh bread, it smelled amazing, and then Fairy Caoimhe brought two bowls of steaming hot soup while the red haired fairy went and got the third bowl. When the three bowls were in front of them Fidelma found herself taking a moment to inhale the delicious fragrance before picking up her spoon and making a start on the soup, it was perfect.

After lunch Cailte Mac Ronan stood up from the table and excused himself "Come on Fidelma, we have lots to do" Fidelma smiled and stood up. "Once you are finished with Cailte Fidelma you can go home, you are going to be exhausted." said Fairy Áine. Fidelma nodded, she was tired already, the archery lessons were intense and after two helpings of the delicious soup and lots of beautiful bread, all she wanted to do was lie down, but as Cailte said, they had lots to do.

The unlikely pair took a walk through the field outside An Crann darach Sean. Cailte talked as they walked "So Fidelma, when speaking with animals they mostly understand our vowels, I am going to teach you a few basic words, however, mostly when I converse with the animals, it is through my mind" he glanced at Fidelma who was now frowning "Your mind?" she asked sceptically, Cailte smiled "Yes, that cannot be taught, it is a gift, bestowed upon me and very few others but a gift that your Grandmother possessed, and her grandmother before her so we are optimistic that you too have this special gift" Fidelma stopped walking and shook her head "No, I definitely do not have that gift, I think I would know if I could telepathically speak to animals" Cailte just smiled gently "No Fidelma, you would not, we won't know if you have the gift until I sit with you,

the gift needs to be released" Fidelmas face was a picture, Cailte gave a little laugh and continued "You will see, trust me, now come on, we are going to see the lovely Dílis."
And they walked on.

Dílis was happily grazing when Cailte and Fidelma approached. As they got closer he stopped and looked up. Cailte simply raised his hand; Dílis let out a low rumbly neigh and seemed to nod his head. "Now" said Cailte to Fidelma "Dílís has just said he is happy to see you again" Fidelma beamed in surprise "Oh really?" she exclaimed as she rubbed Dílís nose affectionately. "He is very fond of you Fidelma and thinks you two are going to make a great team" said Cailte as he opened his hand under Dílís mouth, Fidelma watched as Dílís pressed his long nose into Cailtes shovel like hand to devour the oats in it before Cailte stuck his hand into his satchel and produced another handful this time handing them to Fidelma "Here" he gestured to her "cup your hands together." Fidelma did as she was asked and Cailte emptied the oats into her hands. "Go ahead" said Cailte pointing his head towards Dílís "Feed your horse." Fidelma carefully raised her cupped hands towards Dílís and her horse promptly nuzzled in and began to gobble up the oats, Fidelma giggled as she felt his tongue tickle her palm. Cailte rubbed Dílis on the nose affectionately "Good boy Dílis, good boy" "So Fidelma" he said "Without the gift, you can speak to Dílis now and he will understand you however until we release your gift he will not be able to speak to you, or should I say, you will not be able to hear him." Fidelma looked from one to the other and simply nodded, she had no words, her brain was scrambling to say something but this was not a normal situation. "Come" continued Cailte "let us sit over here under that tree and talk some more." Fidelma followed Cailte to a nearby tree where they both sat down, Cailte was sitting cross legged so Fidelma sat facing him in the same position, she watched as Cailte began to take deep breaths and wring his hands loosely by their wrists. "Try to relax your mind Fidelma" he said gently "Do as I do, close your eyes, take deep breaths in and let them out slowly" Fidelma did as she was asked, after a moment Cailte spoke in a quiet soothing voice "now, keeping your eyes closed, place your hands palms down gently beside you on the grass, take a deep breath, in. . . . out. . . in . . . out . .

good. Now without moving your hands, *feel* the grass beneath them, just feel it, the grass has an energy" Cailtes spoke in a calm soothing hypnotic voice "just relax and picture the grass, breathe in and out, smell the grass, take in its energy" Fidelma was feeling completely relaxed, she felt like she was drifting off into another world.

Cailte slowly moved forward and pressed the palm of his hand on Fidelmas forehead, she was so relaxed she didn't even flinch. Cailte whispered "Scaoil an fuinneamh" his other hand was now clenching the grass, this time he spoke much louder "Scaoil an fuinneamh!" Fidelma fell backwards onto the soft grass. "Oh" she yelped, startled "What happened?"

Cailte stood up smiling, he put his hand out to Fidelma and pulled her up onto her feet "I think your gift has just been released Fidelma" he said patting her on the back "it did not take long at all, your gift is strong" Fidelma just stared at him bewildered, suddenly she jumped as she heard another voice "Any more oats?" Fidelma spun around to find nobody else there, she suddenly felt scared "Who's there?" she said "Who said that?"

Cailte gently placed his hand on Fidelmas arm and guided her towards Dilís. Cailte spoke with a smile "Who do you think is looking for more oats Fidelma?" Fidelmas hand flew to her mouth in shock "What?" she asked "he spoke? Dilís actually spoke?" Cailte shrugged "Sort off, he did not speak as you and I would speak, but he is wondering if we have any more oats for him so he used his mind to ask" Fidelma looked from Cailte to Dilís and back to Cailte, she knew what this lesson was, Fairy Áine had explained she would learn how to converse with animals, but honestly? Nothing could have prepared her for hearing her new horse speak directly to her, it was mind-blowing. She had so many questions, she started with the first one "How do I speak back to him?" "Easy" started Cailte "you just think what you want to say to him, arrange it into a sentence and say it in your mind, but you need to direct it to Dilís or you will have every animal in the country replying to you" Again, Fidelma looked from one to the other before speaking "Ok, so how do I direct it to just Dilís" Cailte opened his hand for Dilís to eat more oats as he spoke "Practice Fidelma, plenty of practice, but do not worry, it will come to you, it is a very special gift, and one that will be with you in your own world too so be aware of that" Fidelma simply nodded, she could not really get her head around this, she was completely overwhelmed and Cailte could tell by her dazed expression. "Okay" he said "come on, let's get you back so you can go home, I think a good rest is in order, you have had quiet the day Fidelma." Fidelma nodded "I am exhausted" Cailte turned to make his way back towards An Crann Darach Sean "Of course you are, you have just released a magnificent gift, it takes a lot out of you" Fidelma smiled and began to walk with him, in her mind she said "good talking to ye Dilís" without even thinking and almost immediately she heard her loyal horse "Until next time Fidelma". She was startled and stopped in her tracks, Cailte patted her gently on the back "Well done Fidelma, that was great" Fidelma smiled and gave Dilís a wave.

Chapter 16

Fidelma was sitting on the bench in her back garden reading one of the books she picked up in the library when her Mother interrupted her "Fidelma don't forget to pack a bag later" Fidelma was completely engrossed in her book "hmmm?" she replied looking up at her Mam. Mrs. Doyle shook her head as she pegged clothes on the washing line "our weekend away Fidelma? The hotel in West Meath near that lake you and your father wanted to go to?" Fidelma shut her book "Oh yes Mam of course, I hadn't forgotten, I'm looking forward to it" Mrs. Doyle smiled "Ah it'll be lovely, this weather is supposed to keep up over the weekend so make sure you pack accordingly"

Fidelma went up to her bedroom, she took a bag down from the top of her wardrobe and opened it up on her bed, she opened a couple of drawers and began taking out shorts and t-shirts, folding them and putting them into her bag, she went back to her wardrobe and took out a pair of jeans when she heard a strange voice, it seemed to be screeching "Stay away! Stay away!" Fidelma froze for a moment while she tried to work out where the voice was coming from, it sounded like it was coming from her front garden, she walked over to the window and looked out but could not see anyone. "That's strange" she thought to herself as she stood scanning the street, it happened so quickly Fidelma jumped backwards screaming, a large black crow came flying at the window and began banging at the pane with its beak, it seemed to be cawing loudly, but Fidelma suddenly realised she could understand the crow, "Stay away, or you will be sorry" it was screeching, Fidelma felt petrified as she realised this was obviously the same crow that had attacked her, she quickly drew the curtains, after a moment the screeching stopped. Just as Fidelma sat down on her bed her Mother walked in, she could see her daughter was visibly shaken, "Fidelma! What's wrong" asked Mrs. Doyle as she walked towards the bed. Fidelma shook her head "Nothing Mam why?" "Why?" asked Mrs. Doyle "because I could've sworn I heard you scream, then I come upstairs to find you in a state" Fidelma laughed unconvincingly "Mam, I'm not in a state, I'm packing my bag" Mrs. Doyle looked over at the window "Why are the curtains pulled?" Fidelma shrugged. Mrs. Doyle walked over and opened the curtains, she jumped as she did, there, still perched on the window sill was the crow, it began its relentless banging and screeching again, Mrs. Doyle stepped back from the window and looked at Fidelma, who shrugged again "now you know why I had the curtains pulled" Mrs. Doyle stared at her daughter for a moment before going back to the window and banging her fist on it "Shoo ye big ugly bird, shoo!" she went to open the window, knocking against the crow, the bird flapped its large wings and took off. Fidelma walked over to her Mam "You showed him Mam" Mrs. Doyle put her arm around her daughter "Jeez I don't know what that birds problem is Fidelma, I'll speak to your Father later, he'll know what to do, never seen the likes of it!" Fidelma muttered "Me neither", her Mother looked at her then gave her a hug "It's alright love it's gone now, ye should've called me, sure that thing would scare the living daylights out of ye cawing and banging like that" Fidelma smiled at her Mother, God she loved her.

Chapter 17

Later that evening Fidelma was finishing her dinner, she was sitting at the table in the kitchen with her parents and Sean, it was nice, Sean worked long hours and wasn't always home to have dinner with the rest of them so Fidelma was always happy when it happened, she got on well with her big brother. Mrs. Doyle spoke to her husband "We had another visit from our bird friend today", Mr. Doyle looked up from his plate, fork halfway towards his mouth "Ye what? Are you serious?" Sean was curious now "What's this" he asked his Mother. Mrs. Doyle turned to her son "Fidelma had a bit of a run in with a crow the other day" Sean looked from his Mother to his sister, Fidelma smiled wryly and showed him her cut hands, Sean looked confused "What" he asked "did ye fall?" Mrs. Doyle answered "No, the crow attacked her, drew blood". Once again Sean looked from his Mother to his sister, trying to understand "It attacked your hands?" he asked. Fidelma shook her head "It was going for my head so I put my hands over it for protection, it was mad". Mrs. Doyle piped in "Frightened the life out of her so it did". Sean was staring at Fidelmas hands in shock, he pointed at them with his forkful of food "And the crow done that to ye?" Fidelma smiled and nodded "yeah, it was pretty aggressive" Sean shook his head "Get a sling and some pellets that'll sort it out." Mr. Doyle coughed and spluttered as he sipped his water "Jaysis Sean will ye stop, ye can't be at that now, there has to be more to it, google it Fidelma, we didn't disrupt a nest or anything did we?" Fidelma giggled "No Dad, it's been a while since I climbed a tree"

✶✶✶✶✶✶

After dinner Fidelma had gone to her room to read, she was lying on her bed reading through one of the books from the library, still trying to make some sense of the tragedy of the children of Lír. The sun was starting to set so Fidelma got up to close the curtains, she had a little look out of the window for the crow but there was no sign, maybe it had given up, she turned on her bedside lamp and sat back down on her bed, she knew any minute now Fairy Áine would come for her, she wondered would she get to see Dilís today, she couldn't wait, even though this job of being Fairy Protector was tough, it was definitely worth it, she was one lucky girl!

The Treasure Chest began to rattle and out popped the now familiar flash of light, bouncing around the room before landing on the bed beside her, Fidelma briefly wondered if Fairy Áine actually had to bounce around like that or did she simply do it for a bit of fun.

"Dia dhuit Fidelma" Fairy Áine flew up and kissed her on the tip of her nose.

"Dia dhuit mo chara" replied Fidelma, Fairy Áine smiled and held out her hand.

Chapter 18

Fidelma was sitting at the table in An Crann Darach Sean with Fairy Caoimhe drinking tea. Fairy Caoimhe was regaling Fidelma with tales of her Grandmother. "What was Grannys horse called" Fidelma asked, delighted to be hearing stories of her beloved Granny. Fairy Caoimhe smiled "Ámharach, it means lucky" Fidelma closed her eyes and smiled as she tried to imagine

Granny with Ámharach "Well he certainly was lucky, I'd say my Granny loved him" Fairy Caoimhe nodded "oh she did, they became extremely close, from what I remember your Grandmother took great comfort from Ámharach when she was here, there were some problems with life in her world, I recall one occasion when I heard her pleading with Queen Áine to allow her to live here permanently, she was sobbing, but the Queen was adamant that *her* world must always be her home" The two were interrupted suddenly by Fairy Áines sharp voice "Fairy Caoimhe!" Fairy Caoimhe jumped up from the table looking flustered, she lifted her cup and bowed to her Queen "I beg your pardon Queen Áine, Fidelma and I were just chatting" "So I heard" replied Fairy Áine curtly, "Please go and prepare Dilís for our journey" Fairy Caoimhe simply bowed her head again and left the room silently. Fidelma wasn't too sure what just happened but she knew that it made her feel uncomfortable. Fairy Áine looked at her for a moment before she spoke "Come young Fidelma, we must get you ready for our trip, we will go to your room and I will help you pack." Fidelma nodded and followed the Fairy down the hallway to her room.

✶✶✶✶✶✶

Fidelma was all packed and ready to go, she was walking with Fairy Áine towards Dilís where Fairy Caoimhe was waiting with him. Fidelma found herself automatically saying "*Hello Dilís*" in her mind as she raised her hand to wave to him, he neighed and nodded his head but to Fidelmas delight she heard his reply as clear as day; "*Hello Fidelma, so happy to see you.*" Fidelma gave a little giggle, Fairy Áine who was fluttering along beside her shoulder looked at her "Did you understand him?" she asked, Fidelma nodded grinning from ear to ear, putting her arms around the horse when she reached him. The two fairies looked at each other and smiled, they had definitely chosen well with Dilís, the right horse was so important for the Fairy Protector.

"Fidelma" announced Fairy Áine "We are heading now to Loch Dearg to visit Bodb Dearg, I need to warn you that this journey could be dangerous which is why you have your bow and arrows but most importantly you will need your wits about you, Dilís is fully trained for journeys like this, he will be loyal to you from now until the day he dies and will undoubtedly save your life on numerous occasions" Fidelma stood silently listening to the Queen, her heart was pounding, was she scared? Too right she was scared. Was she excited? Well, yes, she did feel a bit excited too; this was going to be like no other trip she'd ever taken that was for sure. Fidelma thought about the 'travel clothes' she was wearing, the satchel she carried across her body along with her Quiver loaded with arrows. She also had a sort of leather contraption strapped over her shoulder which she still hadn't worked out its purpose. All she could think of was what would Aaron say if he seen her right now, she bit her lip to hold in a giggle that was threatening to escape. Fairy Áine continued talking "We still don't know what awaits us Fidelma but I do know that Bodb Derg is a good man so *he* is not to be feared, however we need to be prepared for all eventualities, make no mistake young Fidelma, I could not make this journey without you, after all, you are my protector!" Fidelma gulped at the enormity of the Queens words; Fairy Áine smiled "My protector and my friend of course. Now you're probably wondering what the strap on your shoulder is for?" Fidelma simply nodded and Fairy Áine flew towards her, onto her shoulder and sat into the little 'contraption'. Wow, it was like a little seat strapped to Fidelmas shoulder, she hadn't even realised that was what it was, it was fascinating, these fairies were so inventive thought Fidelma, she also thought that she was glad to have Fairy Áine so close to her as she climbed up on Dilís. Fairy Caoimhe fluttered up and gave Fairy Áine a hug "Bí cúramach anois!" she said to her Queen before fluttering up to kiss Fidelma on the cheek and then to kiss Dilís on the nose "Please come back safely my friends" she called as she turned to fly back towards An Crann darach Sean. Fidelma and Fairy Áine waved as they set off.

Chapter 19

Fidelma guessed they had been travelling for about an hour, with Fairy Áine sitting safely on her shoulder she was able to give directions into Fidelmas ear as well as chat companionably, now she directed Fidelma to slow down and guide Dilís to their right. "There's a stream just over here" said the fairy "Dilís can get a drink and we can stretch our legs for a bit"

They came to the stream and Fidelma climbed down while Fairy Áine undid her safety straps. Fidelma done a couple of stretches then walked over to where Dilís was drinking from the stream, she rubbed his neck *"Good boy, you must've been thirsty"* "Very" came his simple reply as he carried on drinking. Fidelma looked over at Fairy Áine, she was crouched down at the stream, cupping water in her hands and splashing it on her face, Fidelma went and sat down beside her "So refreshing" said the fairy "you should try it Fidelma" Fidelma kneeled over the water and scooped some up with her hands and splashed it over her face,

Fairy Áine was right, it was so refreshing. Fidelma took her canteen out of her satchel and filled it with fresh water. "So" she began as she sat on the grass beside her fairy companion "have we much father to go?" Fairy Áine shook her head "No Fidelma, we have the bulk of the journey done, not too far to go now" "Oh great" smiled Fidelma, relieved. "We just follow the stream now" said Fairy Áine "This stream flows from Loch Dearg and there we will find Bodbs kingdom" Fidelma picked at the grass and daisies beside her "What's he like?" she asked. "Bodb?" asked the fairy "Well he is an enormously imposing figure that's for sure, with bright red hair and a beard to match, he is extremely powerful but he is also wise and very kind" Fairy Áine stood up "come on, let's get going again"

Fidelma stood up and dusted herself off, Dilís was finished drinking and was ready to get going, the trio headed off again along the stream. They were travelling steadily so Fidelma chose this moment to ask Fairy Áine something that had been niggling at her "Fairy Áine can I ask you something" she ventured. "Always Fidelma" replied the fairy adding cautiously "although I cannot promise

I will always be able to answer" "It's about my Granny" started Fidelma "Fairy Caoimhe said she had problems when she was younger" "That's right" said Fairy Áine simply "Fairy Caoimhe did say that, I heard her myself" Fidelma frowned, she could tell Fairy Áine was avoiding the question, she was thinking how to reply when her thoughts were interrupted by the voice of Dilís *"Fidelma I think we have company"* Fidelmas heart skipped a beat *"What do you mean Dilís, what sort of company? I don't see anyone"* Dilís had slowed right down *"The evil kind, I don't know who or what, I cannot see them, but I can sense they are near"*

Fairy Áine knew straight away something was up "What is it Fidelma, what's wrong?" Fidelma was looking all around her "It's Dilís" she said to the fairy "He says he can sense we have company, evil company" Dilís had completely stopped now, Fidelma and Fairy Áine were looking all around them when suddenly there was a deathly silence and a shadow came over the land around them, Fidelma felt the hairs stand on the back of her neck, she noticed the same with Dilís so she rubbed his neck soothingly. Fairy Áine whispered to Fidelma "Fidelma, guide Dilís to our left, there's a forest over there we can take cover in"

"Now?" asked Fidelma, Fairy Áine looked over her shoulder and shouted "Now Fidelma! Go!" They took off in the direction of the forest, Dilís galloping as fast as his legs would carry him, Fidelma hunched forward her heart pounding and Fairy Áine holding on tight as she watched behind her. "Hurry Fidelma, hurry!" she screamed. "What?" panicked Fidelma "Fairy Áine what is it?" *"Dilís you need to go faster buddy"* Fairy Áine clutched her tiny hands onto Fidelmas top as she screamed back "A flying black beast Fidelma! A flying black beast!"

Chapter 20

Dilís came to a stop once they were safely inside the forest, Fidelma was shaking, she was terrified and all she could think of was that *she* was meant to be the protector!

The forest was dark and spookily quiet when suddenly they heard a whooshing sound overhead; Fairy Áine looked at Fidelma and put her finger on her lips before Fidelma could say anything, the whooshing noise got closer, Fidelma looked upwards, the tall trees were blocking the sky but she knew that beyond those dark leaves was the flying beast, she could hear its enormous wings beating. The trio kept perfectly still and quiet when all of a sudden the beast let out an almighty roar, Fidelmas hand flew to her mouth in utter disbelief and tears sprang to her eyes, she quickly hoisted her bow and prepared it with an arrow, she was aiming it upwards, hands shaking, Fairy Áine didn't know what was going on, she undid her straps and stood up on Fidelmas shoulder, leaning against her ear "Fidelma! Fidelma what are you doing? What's wrong? Tell me" Fidelma was trembling as she pointed the arrow in different directions trying to work out where exactly she might aim to result in her hitting the beast when all of a sudden the whooshing noise seemed to move, it was getting further away and the sun began streaming through the leaves down onto the forest floor again, they were still for a moment until they heard birds begin to sing again and the forest seem to come back to life, the beast was gone.

Fidelma relaxed her arms; she turned to look at Fairy Áine who was watching her with concern. "Fidelma, please, talk to me, what just happened?" pleaded the fairy, a tear trickled from Fidelmas eye and made its way down her face leaving a wet streak behind, Fairy Áine watched it until it dripped off Fidelmas chin "Fidelma?" she probed gently, Fidelma looked at her hands for a moment, then she showed them to Fairy Áine "Remember my hands were bandaged?" the fairy nodded, "I got attacked by a crow, an abnormally large black crow outside my house" Fairy Áine took a deep breath "Ok" she said slowly, Fidelma continued "every time I looked out my window it was there, watching me, banging it's beak against my window and screeching, but then . . . then after Cailte released my gift, it came again and instead of hearing it screeching I heard it scream 'stay away, stay away or you'll be sorry'!" Fidelma looked at Fairy Áine, the little fairy began fluttering backwards and forwards trying to make sense of what Fidelma had just told her, she stopped and turned towards Fidelma "What are you thinking, do you think it's something to do with the beast?" Fidelma closed her eyes before she answered "When the beast roared" she said "It was saying the same thing, it said 'stay away, stay away Fidelma or you'll be sorry', it actually said my name" her eyes welled up with tears again; Fairy Áine could tell she was clearly shaken. She stared at Fidelma for a moment, she had a feeling that this was serious and she could tell Fidelma could feel it too; she needed to speak with Bodb Derg. "Fidelma" said the Fairy gently as she flew up close to Fidelmas face, she touched the wet streak and wiped it with her tiny hand, then she leaned in and planted a tiny kiss on Fidelmas cheek, "please do not be scared, I'm here, Dilís is here, you handled that really well, but we need to get to Bodb Derg now, are you ok to keep going?" Fidelma took a deep breath and nodded *'C'mon Dilís let's go'*. The loyal horse turned around and made his way back out of the forest, Fidelma squinted as they emerged in the bright sunlight again *'follow the stream Dilís'* Dilís answered gently *'Fear not Fidelma, I will take good care of you'*. Fidelma gave a watery smile and patted her horse.

After about 15 minutes they came to a lake "Loch Dearg?" asked Fidelma, "Loch Dearg" replied the fairy, "Bodb's castle isn't far from here, you can see the top of it beyond the village to the left." Dilís made his way in the direction of the castle, there were villagers going about their business, nobody took too much notice of them as they passed. Eventually they came to the entrance of the castle; Fidelma climbed down and led Dilís over to graze on some straw with a couple of other horses *'here ye go Dilís, relax and make some friends'* Dilís turned to look at Fidelma *'Thank you, I already know these two'* Fidelma smiled and patted him, it was nice to smile again. She walked towards the two guards that were guarding the entrance, Fairy Áine fluttering along beside her, this time Fidelma spoke clearly and confidently before Fairy Áine had a chance to; "Fidelma Protector of Fairies and Fairy Áine Queen of Fairies to see Bodb Derg" The guards simply nodded and stood aside. Fidelma made her way under the thick stone archway which was the entrance way to the castle "Well done Fidelma, you are really getting the hang of this" Fairy Áine said in a quiet voice, Fidelma smiled back at her fairy friend. They walked down a long stone corridor much like the one at King Lírs, lit by candles on either side of them, at the end was a large wooden door, Fairy Áine flew slightly ahead and Fidelma followed, when they came to the door Fidelma knocked, after a moment the door was opened by a servant, a very short skinny woman with skin so wrinkly she reminded Fidelma of her friends new pug whose little face was all wrinkled up.

"Yes?" spoke the woman, Fidelma answered the woman the same way she did the guards "Fidelma Protector of Fairies and Fairy Áine Queen of fairies here to see Bodb Derg" The woman, who was so short she only came to Fidelmas waist looked up now and seemed to notice Fairy Áine for the first time "Your majesty!" she exclaimed before bowing "I did not see you, please forgive me, it is my pleasure to welcome you" she stood back and opened the door wide for them to enter.

Fidelma entered a large room, the first thing she saw was a large throne, it seemed to be made of gold and the seating was a rich emerald green material, around the dark stone walls hung medieval style banners, they were mostly green and gold in their colours but each had a different design and seemed to tell a story of battles and triumphs. There was another wooden door to the side of where the throne sat which Fidelma hadn't noticed until now when it opened and a man walked in, he was extremely tall and seemed to be wider than any human Fidelma had ever seen without actually been fat, his hair was a fiery red as was his long beard, Fidelma briefly remembered seeing him at the wedding of King Lír and Aoife. The imposing figure walked straight towards them, Fairy Áine fluttered in front of Fidelma and bowed to Bodb Derg so Fidelma done the same. Bodh Derg waved his hand dismissing them of their courtesy "You're welcome, you're welcome, thank you for coming, come" he turned on his heel and headed back towards the door he had just come through, Fidelma and Fairy Áine followed. They stepped through to another room, as big as the last but taken up by a long table surrounded by a dozen or so regal looking high backed chairs, at the top of the table was a slightly smaller version of the throne from the other room, this was where Bodh headed and he motioned for Fidelma to take a seat close to him. As Fidelma took her seat she noticed on the table a tiny version of the throne, Fairy Áine sat straight into it without batting an eyelid. There were 2 goblets which Bodh proceeded to fill with water from a jug on the table. The servant who had let them in then arrived with a tray, she laid the table with plates for Fidelma and Bodb, a bowl with some chunks of bread, a plate of cheese and another plate of meat which Fidelma wasn't too sure of, she then disappeared. Bodh gestured towards the food and nodded to Fidelma "Please, eat, you must be hungry, please eat." With that the servant re-appeared with another tray, Fidelma watched with amazement as she produced a fairy sized table which she sat beside Fairy Áine and laid it with fairy sized bread, cheese, meat and a goblet of water, Fairy Áine thanked the servant then winked at Fidelma as she caught her staring.

Fidelma took some bread and cheese and put them on her plate, she looked at Bodh Derg who was devouring his food and took some bites herself, it was delicious, why was food so nice in Old Ireland she wondered. After a moment

Fairy Áine spoke "Bodh you know why we are here." Bodh placed his hands palms down on the table and took a deep breath before answering "I know why you are here Fairy Áine, I know why you are here. I wish I had the power to turn back the time, I would never offer Aoife as a wife to Lír, I hold myself responsible for what she has done to those children, I hold myself responsible" Fairy Áine shook her head "You must not blame yourself Bodh, yourself and King Lír blaming yourselves is not going to help the children" Bodh took another deep breath before replying, Fidelma was mesmerized by his manner "Forgive me

Fairy Áine, but I always knew there was something about Aoife, she had a wicked way about her even as a child, she was tremendously jealous of Aoibh but I had hoped she would grow out of it, that was what I had hoped, that she would grow out of it, and now look" He shook his head sadly, Fairy Áine looked at Fidelma, she got up from her seat and walked towards Bodh, she sat beside his large hand on the table and placed her tiny hand on it "That does not mean you are to blame" she paused for a moment before continuing "We need your help now though to help us help the children" Bodh nodded "Whatever you need Fairy

Áine, whatever you need" Fidelma spoke this time "Fairy Áine tells me you banished Aoife from your Kingdom?" Bodh Derg looked at Fidelma and raised his fist in the air "I struck her with my Druid Rod and I turned her into a demon of the air and I banished her from my kingdom forever, banished her from my kingdom forever!" he boomed, bringing his fist down on the table making Fidelma and Fairy Áine jump. Fidelma looked at Fairy Áine, she had a feeling things were falling into place but she wasn't sure she was going to like it. Fairy Áine spoke next "Bodh I need you to describe this air demon to me, please" Bodh took a deep breath before speaking "Black, black as night, enormous" (he stretched out his hands to indicate) "and wicked because she is of wicked heart, I could not change that, and although she is of half-blood, she still possesses the magic of the Tuatha Dé Danann, although she is of half-blood, her magic is evil though, because she is of wicked heart." He looked at Fairy Áine, finished with his description but Fariy Áine had another question for him "Bodh does Aoife possess the power to appear in the Ireland of new?" There was silence for a moment while Bodh considered this, Fidelma felt her heart pounding in her chest, she knew what she wanted the answer to be, however she also knew what the answer might well be, Bodh took a deep breath and she knew he was about to reply. "She can enter the New World, but her power will be weakened so she will take a different form, her power will be weakened in the New World" Fidelma swallowed hard "A different form?" she asked, Bodh turned to look at her "A Raven" he answered simply "A wicked raven." Fairy Áine watched Fidelma as she took in this answer, she was nodding as if this was all perfectly normal, then she looked at her hands where the scratches had begun to heal and Fairy

Áine could see she was beginning to shake, the fairy flew over to her friend and placed her tiny hands over the cuts "It's ok Fidelma, we will sort this"

Chapter 21

Fidelma walked out of the castle with Fairy Áine by her side after they promised Bodh Derg they would indeed do their upmost to save his grandchildren, but she was feeling a bit dazed, if she thought she was scared of the bird that attacked her outside her house then she was terrified of the flying beast that followed them to the forest, but, if they were both the same creature, then she was absolutely petrified.

The trio set off on their journey back to An Crann darach Sean. There was silence for a while, the only sound was that of Dilís hooves on the grass, Fairy Áine was first to speak "Are you alright Fidelma?" Fidelma was lost in thought, she simply nodded.

******

They arrived back at the old oak tree, Fidelma had hardly spoken the whole journey, she climbed down from Dilís "I'll take him to his field" she said in a quiet voice to Fairy Áine, Fairy Áine smiled gently, she was concerned about Fidelma "we will have tea before you go home." She said simply to her friend.

Fidelma walked with Dilís towards his field, *'you heard something that has caused you concern Fidelma?'* came the voice of her now trusted friend, Fidelma patted her horse affectionately *'you are so wise Dilís, did you enjoy meeting with your old friends?'* She wasn't sure she was ready to talk about what she had just learned. Dilís answered; *'They tell me he repeats himself when he speaks, a result of being hit across the head in battle when he was younger'* Fidelma giggled, jeez she loved this horse, Dilís continued though *'What did he repeat to you Fidelma? He told you something that has upset you'* Fidelma sighed *'That flying beast'* Fidelma began *'Is Aoife, Bodb Derg turned her into an air demon, but she also has the power to appear in the New World, and that's exactly what she has done, she sits outside my house, trying to intimidate me'* Dilís nuzzled his nose against Fidelma *'you have such strength Fidelma, you need to call on this strength, you are a Protector, those cuts on your hands? They are battle scars, you do not need to fear this Aoife, you have the skills to overcome her, you need to believe in yourself'* Fidelma smiled and kissed Dilís neck, he was right, she was given this title of Protector for a reason, she couldn't ask for help against the evil Aoife, it was up to her to defeat her, and defeat her she would. She patted her horse *'Thank you Dilís, see you tomorrow'* Dilís neighed *'Until then'*

Fidelma made her way back towards An Crann darach Sean, Fairy Caoimhe was waiting outside, she smiled as she seen Fidelma approaching, she extended her hand to take Fidelma inside. Once inside Fidelma walked into the main room where Fairy Áine was waiting "We have made some tea Fidelma, take a seat" Fidelma smiled broadly at her fairy friend, she could see she was worried about her. "Fairy Áine" she started "I just want you to know that I'm ok" Fairy Áine stared at her as she continued "I was of course thrown at first by what Bodb Derg revealed, but I am ok, you don't need to worry about me" Fidelma straightend herself as she spoke "I am Fidelma, Protector of Fairies, I will protect you all, I will protect myself, I am strong, I do not fear Aoife, I will defeat her and I will save the children of Lír".

Chapter 22

Fidelmas alarm was going off beside her bed, she reached over and knocked it off, stretched and sat up, she could see the sun streaming through her curtains and smiled, her Mother was right, she had said there was good weather forecast for this weekend. Fidelma slipped her feet into her slippers at the side of her bed and made her way downstairs, she followed the smell of sausages into the kitchen. "Good morning love" said Mrs. Doyle "look, the sun is shining, didn't I tell ye." Fidelma smiled at her mother and sat down at the counter. "Yes Mam, once again you were right about the weather." Mrs Doyle placed a mug in front of Fidelma and lifted the teapot off the stove, she spoke as she poured "I thought some sausage sambos would be nice before we head off, save us stopping on the way." Fidelma poured some milk into her cup "Thanks Mam" she said "Where's Dad?" Mrs. Doyle had started to butter a few slices of bread "Oh he's outside packing up the car" she replied "wants to make sure he's got room for his fishing gear" she rolled her eyes making Fidelma smile again.

★★★★★★

A couple of hours later Fidelma and her parents were pulling up outside the hotel. "Oh Mam this looks lovely" exclaimed Fidelma looking out the backseat window. The hotel did indeed look lovely, one part of it seemed quite new whilst the other part seemed older and built from old stone. Fidelma jumped out of the car, she couldn't wait to explore, she walked towards the older part of the hotel but her thoughts were interrupted by her Father calling her "Fidelma! Fidelma come on, get your bag" Mrs. Doyle was lifting her bag out of the boot of the car as Mr. Doyle was taking his fishing rod out, Fidelma reached for her own bag "Dad you're not taking your fishing stuff into the hotel are you?" she asked slightly disgusted at the thought. "No" replied her Father "I'm just checking they survived the journey alright." Fidelma and her Mother exchanged looks and a giggle.

They got checked in, Mrs. Doyle had booked a double room with a connecting single room, Fidelma was in her element, she walked into her room and plonked down on her bed smiling, it was such a treat to be staying in a hotel, she rubbed her hand along the silky smooth bedspread while taking in her surroundings when she spotted a painting on the wall, she jumped up from the bed and walked over to take a closer look. It was titled **The Children of Lír** and conveyed a striking image of Aoife casting her spell on the children and they morphing into swans, the artist captured the childrens expressions as being terrified and Fidelma felt herself tearing up as she stared at the picture. A few months ago she would barely have noticed this painting, now she wondered how many people had stayed in this room and how many of them had actually noticed it; she imagined if any of them had that they wouldn't have been nearly as affected as she was with the image. Fidelma wiped a tear away with the back of her hand, picked up her bag and threw it down on the bed, she unzipped it and there nestled on top of her clothes was the treasure chest, she carefully lifted it out and placed it beside her bed on the locker, she then had a root in the bag and produced a notebook and pen, she took her small backpack off her back and put the notebook into it, picked her phone up off the locker and zipped it safely into an inside pocket.

Mrs. Doyle was checking out the hotel toiletries and Mr. Doyle was sitting on the bed reading through the menu when Fidelma came into their room, "Right I'm going for a walk" she announced. Mrs. Doyle popped her head out of the bathroom "What? What about lunch?" Fidelma looked at her Father expecting support but he just raised his eyebrows, Fidelma rolled her eyes and picked an apple from the fruit bowl on the small table "I'm not really hungry just yet, I just want to take a little look around, I'll be back in an hour and have lunch then" Mrs. Doyle wagged a bottle of hotel shampoo at her daughter as she spoke "1 o'clock! Be back by 1 and we'll all go for lunch"

Fidelma came out of the lift into the reception area, she walked over to a stand where there were numerous pamphlets and maps, she flicked through them before choosing a handful and popped them into her bag except one which had a map of the area on it. Fidelma smiled at the receptionist as she walked out into the sunshine.

Once outside, Fidelma headed in the direction of the Lake, it was a beautiful day, the sun was shining and there wasn't a cloud to be seen in the sky. The hotel they were staying at wasn't too far from the lake so she didn't have far to walk. As Fidelma approached the area around the lake she could see a caravan park, she took her phone out of her bag and took a photo of it, she was going to show it to her parents, maybe they could camp there next time. Fidelma walked along the outside of the caravan park along a pathway that led down towards the lake, she could hear the sound of children's happy squeals in the distance, it reminded her of being a child and playing outside with her friends in the summertime. She then thought of Aaron and how she missed him while he was staying at his cousins when her phone beeped notifying her of a text message, she opened it up and smiled to see that it was from Aaron, they often laughed at how in tune they were with each other. Fidelma opened up the text to read it;

Hey what you up to? I'm back from my cousins, I called to your house but no answer ☺

Fidelma grinned as she read the text, she was delighted that Aaron was home, she missed him, actually she wished he was here, he would love it, but then she frowned, no, she had work to do. Fidelma had come to the edge of the lake; she lifted her phone and took a photo of the view then sent it to Aaron with a short text;

Away with the folks for a couple of days, will see you when we get back on Sunday ☺

Fidelma pressed send and stuck her phone in her pocket as she walked closer to the lakes shore, she got down on her hunkers and looked out across the water, she picked up a handful of pebbles and began skimming them across the water when from behind a bed of reeds came a beautiful swan.

Fidelma was transfixed by it, she watched as the graceful bird glided through the water towards her, she spoke absently to the creature "Sorry Mr swan, I don't have any bread." Fidelma stumbled backwards with shock and landed on her bum when she heard the swan reply to her in a sweet voice *"It's ok Fidelma I am not looking for food, and it's not Mr. Swan, it's me. . . Fionnuala"* Fidelma stumbled back onto her feet, she dusted herself off and looked around her to see if anyone was watching, but there was nobody around apart from a boat far out on the lake. Fidelma bent down and spoke quietly to the swan *"Fionnuala I.. I* don't understand, why. . . how did you get here?" The swan came closer to Fidelma "*I cannot stay long Fidelma, I have just come to warn you, you need to watch out for Aoife, she is of wicked heart, she knows you are trying to help us and she will do whatever she can to stop you*" Fidelma rubbed her forehead as she took this in "*Fionnuala please don't worry about me, I will do whatever **I** can to save you and your brothers, I am a Protector, it's very good of you to come but really you need to stay with your brothers, try not to put yourself in any unnecessary danger.*" The beautiful swan bowed her graceful neck as she replied *"You do not understand Fidelma, Aoife has paid us a visit, she said we are doomed to spend 900 years as swans and she will do whatever it takes to stop anyone who tries to break the spell, especially you Fidelma, she has sent me to warn you"* With that a tear welled up in the swans eyes, Fidelma reached out and touched the birds neck gently *"It's ok Fionnuala, I am not afraid of Aoife, I will find a way to break the spell, trust me. Wait how did you know I was here? Does she know I am here?"* Fionnuala lifted her head and looked up past Fidelma into the trees beyond, she seemed to be focusing on something there. Fidelma turned around to look, there high up in a tree was the wicked Raven, Fidelma felt a shiver go down her spine as they seemed to lock eyes but Fidelma stood up and shouted at the top of her lungs "*I am not afraid of you!*" The raven simply spread its wings and took off in the opposite direction, Fidelma turned and looked at the swan "*I must go, please Fidelma, take care*" and with that she turned around and was gone.

Chapter 23

Fidelma had spent a very enjoyable day with her parents, she had gone straight back to the hotel after her encounter with Fionnuala and had lunch in the restaurant with her Mother and Father, then they had taken a drive into town for a look around, they got dinner while they were in town before making their way back to the hotel. It was almost 7pm when they walked through reception, "Will we go into the bar for a bit?" suggested Mr. Doyle, Mrs. Doyle smiled "Oh yeah sure why not, Fidelma would you fancy a nice Mocktail?" Fidelma faked a yawn "Actually Mam I'm wrecked tired, must be the fresh air, I'm gonna go up and lie down with my book if that's alright?" Mrs. Doyle put her arm around her daughter "If you're sure" she said. "I'm sure" smiled Fidelma. "Well" said Mr. Doyle "you know where we are if you need us or you change your mind."

Fidelma let herself into the bedroom, she walked straight over to the painting and stared at it, she reached up and lightly touched the tortured faces of the children, completely lost in thought, so much so that she didn't even notice the arrival of Fairy Áine. "Legend might tell of 900 years" muttered Fidelma "but not on my watch!" Fairy Áine smiled broadly "Spoken like a true Protector" she exclaimed. Fidelma jumped "Fairy Áine you frightened me, I didn't even know you were there." Fairy Áine fluttered up and kissed Fidelma on the tip of her nose "I know" she winked, "So" continued the little Fairy "tell me, what have you been up to?" Fidelma went over and sat down on the bed, she picked up her backpack and took out her notebook and phone, opening the camera of her phone Fidelma showed Fairy Áine the photo she had taken of the view of the lake "Recognise this?" she asked. Fairy Áine peered at the screen "That's Lake Derravaragh, looks a bit different but it is definitely the same lake" Fidelma smiled "Yep" she said "Lake Derravargh, that's where I went today and guess who I met?" Fairy Áine thought for a moment before she replied "Fidelma I am honestly not sure, I guess anything is possible though" Fidelma closed her phone and placed it beside the Treasure Chest "Well" she started "I was at the lake basically just gathering my thoughts when all of a sudden a swan appeared" "A swan?" asked Fairy Áine surprised. "Yeah but not just any swan" answered Fidelma "It was Fionnuala!" Fairy Áines wings began to flutter "What?" she exclaimed "Fionnuala? What was she doing here? In the New World? That could have been extremely dangerous for her, why was she here? What did she say?" Fidelma nodded "I know" she said "I did tell her it was dangerous for her to be here but she said she had to come and warn me about Aoife, apparently Aoife paid the children a visit saying that I wouldn't be able to break the spell and she would do whatever it takes to stop me, she told Fionnuala to warn me" Fairy Áine stared at Fidelma in disbelief, after what seemed like an age she put out her tiny hand and spoke "Right Fidelma, come on, we have got work to do!"

Chapter 24

Fidelma was sitting at the table in An Crann Darach Sean with Fairy Áine, Fairy Caoimhe and Fairy Eimear; the three fairies were listening intently to Fidelma as she retold the story of Fionnualas visit. When she finished there was silence for a moment, Fairy Eimear was the first to speak "And what about Aoife? Have you seen her since?" Fidelma had been so caught up talking about seeing Fionnuala that she had forgotten to mention the wicked ravens' appearance. "Actually" started Fionnuala, looking over at Fairy Áine "When I asked Fionnuala if

Aoife knew where I was she looked up into some trees and there on a treetop was Aoife in her raven form." Fairy Áine stood up "Fidelma" she announced in shock "Why didn't you mention this earlier? Did she attack you again?" Fidelma shook her head "No" she replied "That's just it, she just sat there on the branch, staring at me, it was quite un-nerving actually, and then after a minute or two she just took off." The fairies all exchanged looks "She just took off?" asked Fairy Eimear, Fidelma simply nodded. "Did she fly at you? Or say anything to you?" asked Fairy Caoimhe. Fidelma shook her head "No" she answered

"Nothing, like I said she just stared and then she was gone, actually the more I think of it now it was pretty strange." Fidelma watched as Fairy Áine began to pace and the other two fairies exchanged looks. "What?" asked Fidelma "What is it? Fairy Áine what do you think it means?" Fairy Caoimhe got up from the table and fetched some more tea, Fairy Áine stopped pacing, she stood in front of Fidelma resting her hands on the table as she spoke "Fidelma, Aoife is out to get you, she knew where you were but yet she did not attack you." Fidelma frowned, she was confused "I don't understand Fairy Áine" she said "Why are you worried, isn't it a good thing that she didn't attack me?" Fairy Áine shook her head "Fidelma you don't understand, she must be up to something, she has already attacked you in your world, she waited outside your house and tried to intimidate you." Fidelma didn't get what Fairy Áine was getting at "I know Fairy Áine" she exclaimed "I know, and she has failed, she has tried her best to scare me but I am not afraid and I told her as much, I am the Protector it will take more than a raven to scare me!" Fairy Áine was shaking her head, Fidelma frowned. Fairy Caoimhe arrived with fresh tea, there was silence for a moment before

Fairy Áine spoke "Fidelma, Aoife knows that attacking you in your world has not worked, shouting at you outside your house has not worked, sending Fionnuala to warn you off has not worked" Fairy Áine took a breath before she continued "She will now try something new, she will try and get to you in another way, I wish I knew how exactly but all I know is that she will stop at nothing." Fidelma did not like the sound of this, she was starting to get worried "What exactly are you saying Fairy Áine?" Fairy Áine looked at the other fairies as she sat back down, she reached her hands across the table and took Fidelmas hands in hers "Fidelma" she started "I cannot say for sure but there is a chance Aoife will go after your loved ones, your family!" Fidelma gulped, she actually felt like she might be sick, she had found the strength within that Dilís had spoken of, she was willing to take on Aoife and whatever else she would be confronted with, what she was not prepared for though was putting her family in danger, she simply could not bare it if being the Protector brought danger to her loved ones. Fairy Áine interrupted her thoughts. "Fidelma" she said quietly "We should go to Lake Derravaragh now and see the children" she turned to Fairy Coimhe "Can you prepare Dilis please?" Fairy Caoimhe simply nodded and scurried away as Fairy Áine turned to Fairy Eimear "We will need travel clothes and some food please."

******

Fidelma, Fairy Áine and Dilís had been travelling for a while before they stopped for a break, Fidelma guided Dilís towards a small stream where she climbed down and Fairy Áine undid her safety straps. Dilís was happy to slurp at the water while Fidelma and Fairy Áine sat themselves down beside him. Fidelma was taking bread and cheese from her satchel when Fairy Áine confided in her "You know Fidelma, there is something I never told you, remember the day I came to see King Lír on my own with Eimhin?" Fidelma nodded as she tore off a piece of bread "Well something strange happened on our way, it was similar to when we were on our way to meet Bodb Derg, except we did not actually see the demon, but we knew she was there, or at least something or someone was there, she was following us." Fidelma took a drink of water from her canteen "Ok" said Fidelma "but I don't understand, why didn't you tell me?" Fairy Áine bowed her head "I did not want to frighten you" she replied in a small voice. "Frighten me?" asked Fidelma "Wait, did you not think I could handle it?" Fairy Áine shrugged, her head still bent. "Fairy Áine!" Fidelma raised her voice slightly "Look at me!" Fairy Áine looked up sheepishly at Fidelma. "Did you think I couldn't handle it?" Dilís lifted his head from the stream and looked at the two unlikely friends, he had not heard the conversation but he could feel the tension. Fairy Áine finally spoke "Fidelma, please do not be cross with me, you were our new Protector, I was still getting to know you, this is a tough job, a sometimes dangerous job, you could have turned your back on it if you wanted to, and I knew that if you were scared then there was a chance you would have a change of mind and. . . well. . . I did not want you to, I like having you as our Protector and I like having you as my friend, please do not be cross with me" pleaded the little Fairy. Fidelma sat for a moment in silence before getting up and walking away; she walked along the stream for a bit before sitting down. Dilís watched Fidelma then turned and looked over at Fairy Áine, the little Fairy stood up and fluttered over to her friend, she landed down on Fidelmas knee and looked up at her. Fidelma sighed "It's not that I am cross with you, I'm disappointed." Fairy Áine hung her head as Fidelma continued "I have put my trust in you, in all of you, you take me here and tell me that it is my job to protect you and your friends and I just went along with it, do you know why? Because I trusted you! Now if I am to do my job properly I need you to trust me too!" Fairy Áine wiped a tiny tear from her eye "I do trust you Fidelma, honestly I do, it was a bad judgement on my behalf and I am sorry, please forgive me, I promise I won't keep anything from you again!" Fidelma looked at the little fairy for a moment before smiling "Of course I forgive you" Fairy Áine flew up and kissed Fidelma on the tip of her nose, Fidelma continued "Please don't keep anything else from me, we could have known that Aoife was following us sooner." Fairy Áine was contrite "I know Fidelma, I truly am sorry" she fluttered up in front of Fidelma "We should get going."

Chapter 25

Finally they arrived at Lake Derravaragh, Fidelma could see the 4 swans huddled together at the edge of the lake with a human figure, as they arrived she realised the figure was that of King Lír. Fidelma climbed down off Dilís *"Go get yourself a drink boy"* and she made her way towards Lír, he stood as he seen her approach. Fidelma bowed to him "King Lír" she said. "Fidelma, Fairy Áine, always a pleasure" spoke the King. "Fidelma would like to speak with the children" said Fairy Áine. "Of course" said King Lír "I need to go stretch my legs anyway; I will go for a short walk." Fidelma sat down on the shore, "Fionnuala, boys, it's good to see you getting to spend time with your

Father" said Fidelma, the swans came closer to Fidelma, Fionnuala was the first to speak in her sweet sing song voice "Fidelma thank you for coming to see us" Fidelma smiled "You're welcome Fionnuala, I just have a few questions if that's alright?" Fionnuala looked at her brothers then bowed her graceful neck. Fidelma looked at Fairy Áine before she spoke "Fionnuala I want to help you and your brothers, now the only way I can see of doing that is by breaking the spell so I need to know more about what happened that day, please." Fionnualas eyes welled up with tears as she began her tale "As you know Fidelma, we were uncomfortable around Aoife, when we were with Father she was nice but when we were on our own with her she would say cruel words that hurt us, but when she suggested she take us to see our Grandfather we were not worried, we love our Grandfather and we know that he loves us so we were looking forward to the trip" Fionnuala bowed her head again as a tear dropped from her eye into the lake, Aodh came closer to Fionnuala and draped his large white wing around his sister "It was an extremely hot day" Aodh continued for her "Aoife took us to this lake and said we could cool down with a swim if we liked, we did like, we loved the water, it was lovely and we were splashing about having fun for a bit when suddenly Aoife began screeching" Fidelma was listening intently "Go on Aodh, what did she say?" Aodh continued "She began saying that our Father did not really love us, that we bored him, that she was all he needed, we protested, Fionnuala told her that he loved us all, us and her and that we could be a family if only she would let us" Aodh shook his head and Fionnuala took up where he left off "She flew into a rage screeching like the banshee, she said she would kill us if it were not for the fact that she knew our ghosts would haunt her forever, before we knew it there was a crack of thunder, she raised her hands in the air screaming, she caught a bolt of lightning with her wand and threw it at us saying we would live our lives as swans for 300 years on this lake, 300 years on the Straits of Moyle and a further 300 on the Isle of Inish Glora!" Fidelma waited for Fionnuala to continue "She said the spell could only be broken when the Man from the North joined the Woman from the South" The four swans huddled together to comfort each other. Fidelma spoke soothingly to them "Children I am sorry if I upset you but you understand I needed to know all the details, it might help work out how to break her spell" Fionnuala swam over to Fidelma and nuzzled her beak against her "It is alright Fidelma" she said quietly "Of course we understand and we know that you will do what you can to help us, we trust you." Fidelma took a deap breath, she felt overwhelmed by Fionnualas words, and she glanced at Fairy Áine who simply smiled and winked at her. Fidelma touched her hand to Fionnualas neck "I won't stop until I break her wicked spell, I promise." Fidelma stood up and made her way over to King Lír "Did you get what you needed?" he asked her. "I did thank you King Lír" replied Fidelma "I promise I will do what I can to save your children; in the meantime I hope the hut is comfortable for you?" "It is" replied the King "and thank you, I know you will save my children, I put my trust in you" Fidelma gave him a watery smile and bowed her head; King Lír bowed his head and walked back to his children.

Fidelma was making her way back to An Crann darach Sean with Fairy Áine. So many thoughts were going through Fidelmas mind, how the children had so much trust in her, would she be able to work out how to break the spell and more worryingly her family and what she would do if anything happened to them. Fairy Áine was quiet too; she knew Fidelma had a lot on her mind so she let her be.

Chapter 26

The next morning Fidelma was woken by Mrs. Doyle coming into her room and opening her curtains "Good morning Fidelma, time to get up sleepy head!" Fidelma groaned as she rolled over to face her Mother "Awww really Mam, what time is it?" Mrs. Doyle smiled "9 o'clock love, your Dad was up at 6 bless him, already away fishing; we'll get breakfast and go for a bit of shopping then meet him at the lake later on. Your Dad says he has a surprise for us." Fidelma sat up and smiled at her Mother "It's ok Mam, you had me at breakfast."

Fidelma was a tad disappointed at their shopping trip, there really wasn't much to choose from in the way of shops, Dublin city this wasn't. Still, she was enjoying just wandering around with her Mother, it was nice. It was midday and Mrs Doyle said she needed to go into the local supermarket "I thought we could get a few bits for a picnic to take to the lake" she said to Fidelma. That sounded like a pretty good plan to Fidelma, they picked up some ready-made salads and drinks then hopped into a taxi to take them to the lake.

When they arrived at Lake Derravaragh Mr. Doyle was sitting on a bench enjoying the view, he stood up when he seen them approach "So how was the shopping?" he asked Fidelma. "Ah it was grand" she replied "Don't worry we didn't do any damage to your credit card" Mr. Doyle laughed "What a relief" he said jokingly. Mrs. Doyle plonked her shopping bag onto the picnic table "I got some salads, some drinks and buns" she said to her husband. The three of them sat down at the table and enjoyed their lunch in the sunshine. "Did you see the caravan park?" Fidelma asked them, she got her phone out as she spoke to show them the photo she had taken, Mrs. Doyle took it from her to have a look. "I spotted it alright" said her Father "I popped in for a look around while I was waiting on you, picked up one of their brochures, it's a lovely spot, they've got mobile homes onsite that you can hire."

After a while Mr. Doyle looked at his watch "Right" he said standing up "let's get this packed up, time for the surprise." Fidelma smiled at her Dad, sometimes his idea of a surprise fell short of impressing anyone else in her family, but she loved him for trying. They made their way back up towards the carpark where there was a small cabin, Mr. Doyle led them over to it, just as they got to it an old man exited through the creaky door, Fidelma looked at him, he had shaggy grey hair and a long grey beard, he wore an old tweed cap and his clothes looked as though they were from an older time. He was puffing on a pipe when he put his hand out to shake Mr. Doyles hand "How's it going?" he said in way of greeting, Mr. Doyle replied and introduced them "Good good thanks, this is my wife Maebh and our daughter Fidelma." They all shook hands and Mr. Doyle turned to Fidelma and his wife "This is your surprise, Mr. O'Neill here is going to give us a tour of the lake, he knows all its history" Mr. Doyle smiled broadly, he was delighted with himself and Mrs. Doyle smiled politely and glanced at Fidelma thinking her teenage daughter would be disappointed but much to her surprise Fidelma seemed absolutely thrilled with the idea. "Please" spoke Mr.

O'Neill to them "call me Pat." "Ok Pat" smiled Fidelma, this was excellent, her Dad had done well on this occassion.

Pat handed each of them a map of the area, on one side was a map of the lake as it was now but on the other side was an old fashioned map which showed the area to be slightly different. Pat seen Fidelma looking at the two different maps and he pointed to the old style one "This one here is what the area was like around three hundred years ago" Fidelma looked at the man "What you think it might have looked like?" she asked him sceptically, "Nope" replied Pat simply "My Grandfather gave me a map of the area that had been in the family for a couple of generations before him so it's pretty accurate, he passed down some folklore to me when he was alive and I would like to share some of them with you today." Fidelma beamed, Mrs. Doyle spoke up "My Mother, Fidelmas Granny, used to tell her old tales too didn't she luv?" But if Mrs. Doyle was trying to impress old Pat it didn't work "Not tales" he said frowning "Folklore!" he turned to Fidelma "Your Granny told you real stories Fidelma didn't she? She wasn't making them up." Fidelma stared at this old man, did he know something? Did he know Granny Fidelma? Or was he just a tad eccentric, suddenly she was aware of her parents staring at her, they were waiting for an answer "Yes" she said "Grannies story were very real." "That's right" said old Pat satisfied, Fidelma looked at her parents and winked, they were happy enough now.

The four of them set off with Pat leading the way, he led them back up through the car park, as they walked Fidelma took her notebook and pen out of her bag. "If you look over there to the east" pointed Pat "those are the Hills of Ranaghan, if you walk through those hills you will find many Fairyforts." Mr. Doyle frowned "Don't you mean Ringforts?" he asked of Pat. "No sir" answered Pat still walking "none believers call them Ringforts, they only think they know what they're talking about, but believe me, they are Fiaryforts." Mr. and Mrs Doyle exchanged looks and raised eyebrows but Fidelma was intrigued "Why did the fairies build the Fairyforts Pat?" she was getting her pen ready to jot down his answer in her notebook. "Protection" answered Pat simply, Mr. Doyle rolled his eyes. "From the new people who arrived on their shores?" asked Fidelma. "That's exactly it

Fidelma, these strangers had never seen fairies or other magical creatures so they were unnecessarily afraid of them which meant they tried to harm them, and well, I think you know the rest Fidelma" Fidelma glanced at her parents, she could tell by their faces though that they thought poor Pat was crazy.

"Have you ever heard of Turgesius?" Pat asked them, Mr. Doyle answered "The Viking?" "The Viking!" answered Pat, he stopped walking and turned to face his little audience "Turgesius the Viking was a famous man so he was, he was a force to be reckoned with"

Fidelma was scribbling in her notepad as she listened "Turgesius arrived in Ireland in the mid-9th century, he had a fleet of 120 ships and he took the settlement of Dublin by force from the native rural community which were living there." Pat paused for a moment, Fidelma stopped writing and looked at him "Did he live here?" she asked. "Not right here" said Pat "but he did have strongholds nearby, just southwest of Lough Lene" and he pointed his arm far out. Fidelmas gaze followed where old Pat was pointing, she was fascinated.

"On the other side of the lake there" said Pat pointing to the opposite side of the lake "that's Knockeyon or the Hill of St. Eyon" Fidelma began scribbling in her notebook again, old Pat continued "Up that hill are the ruins of St. Cauragh's chapel, he built the chapel himself from natural rock and dedicated it to St. Eyon, the ruins of St. Cauraghs well are across from it, you should take a ramble up if you have time, the water from that well is said to have miraculous properties." Mr. and Mrs. Doyle exchanged looks again "Ah I don't think we'll have time for that today Pat." said Mr. Doyle, "maybe another time" added Mrs. Doyle. Pat stared at them both for a moment before focusing on Fidelma "Now Fidelma" he started "you might be interested in this old legend my Grandfather told me, not many people know of it." Fidelma looked at Pat eager to hear the story, pen poised. "You see those hills of Ranaghan, you see the main hill? It was said there was a young girl who lived in the community there and when she was out fishing with her brothers one day she met a boy from Knockeyon, and they fell in love" Mrs. Doyle interrupted him "Ah that's lovely" she said smiling, but Pat spun around and cut her off "No Meabh" he said seriously "No it was not lovely, those two communities were enemies" he turned back to Fidelma "That's how it was back then, the boy lived North of the lake and the girl lived South of the lake, so they used to meet up in secret until one day their Fathers found out" Fidelma stopped writing and looked up at Pat "And what happened?" she asked "They were taken to Coipre mac Cormac" "Who was he?" interrupted Fidelma. "He was the King of Leinster then Fidelma, and he decided that they could never marry, their families would never allow it, and so, as a punishment he turned the two of them into mountains" Mr. Doyle let out a laugh "Mountains? Ah come on now Pat, I think your Grandfather was pulling your leg" Mrs. Doyle nudged her husband but Pat just continued "Your parents are non-believers Fidelma, but you listen very carefully" Pat turned now and gestured towards the two hills on either side of the shore "Hundreds of years ago it was said you could see the shape of a mans face on the hill of Knockeyon and the face of a girl on the main hill of Ranaghan, for eternity they would be facing each other but never joining, a lifetime of torture for the young lovers, time though has eroded the mountains so the faces are no longer visible, now they are simply known as Knockeyon and Ranaghan" Pat paused for effect while Fidelma continued writing, when she had stopped he continued, his eyes locked on Fidelma as he spoke "For a short time though Fidelma they were known as, The Man from the North and the Woman from the South!"

Fidelma actually felt dizzy, she could not believe what old Pat had just told her, she stood frozen on the spot as he walked on a bit, puffing on his pipe "That's what my Grandfather told me anyway" she heard him say.

Chapter 27

Later that evening they were back at the hotel having dinner in the restaurant. "Are you ok Fidelma?" Mrs. Doyle asked her daughter, Fidelma was just pushing the food around her plate, she was completely distracted, "I'm grand Mam, just tired that's all." Mr. Doyle looked up from his food "Did you have a good day?" he asked Fidelma "You seemed to enjoy the tour with Pat." Fidelma took a sip of water "I did Dad thanks, I really enjoyed it." Mr. Doyle smiled at his daughter pleased with himself for organising the tour. "I was surprised to be honest love, I thought you'd be bored" said Mrs. Doyle. Fidelma shook her head "Not at all Mam" she said "I thought Pat was really interesting, I liked him." Fidelma took another forkful of food before putting her fork down on the plate "I'm wrecked" she announced "Do you mind if I go on up to bed? I've still got that book to finish."

Fidelma walked back into her room and sat down on the bed, she took her notebook out of her bag and sat with it in her hand while she waited on Fairy Àine, this evening she was very eager to see her fairy friend.

Fairy Áine appeared in her usual way, startling Fidelma who was lost in thought, Fidelma jumped up "Fairy Áine I've done it! I've actually done it!" Fairy Áine looked at Fidelma bewildered "Hey slow done cailín, what have you done?" Fidelma took a deep breath "I've solved the riddle, I know how to break the spell!" she beamed at her friend. Fairy Áine smiled and held out her hand "Come on so mo chara, we have lots to talk about, Fairy Caoimhe has the tea made, let's go."

Once again Fidelma found herself sitting at the table in An Crann darach Sean, she was on her own while

Fairy Áine gathered some of the other fairies, after a couple of minutes the table was full and Fairy Caoimhe was pouring tea. Fairy Áine took her seat at the top of the table, she raised her arm and there was silence "Alright Fidelma, tell us what you have learned." Fidelma looked around the table; she was surrounded by eager faces of fairies waiting with baited breath to hear if she had indeed solved the riddle of Aoifes cruel spell. Fidelma cleared her throat and began "Right, so today my Father organised for us to have a tour of Lake Derravaragh, the person giving the tour was a lovely old man called

Pat" Fidelma looked thoughtful for a moment "I'm not sure but I think he knew." The fairies all looked at each other; Fairy Eimear spoke first "Knew what Fidelma?" But Fidelma just shrugged her shoulders and shook her head "I honestly don't know" she answered "could he know about me? About here? It felt as if he did, or that he knew my Granny, I don't know, something, I just got a feeling." She looked around her, the fairies had been looking at her but now turned their attention to Fairy Áine, who was frowning "Fidelma" she said "I do not know, that sounds odd, something maybe we should investigate, another time though" and she nodded to Fidelma indicating for her to continue "Yes of course" said Fidelma "So Pat told me that he was told stories by his Grandfather, the same way *my* Granny told *me* stories, he told us a few but the important one he told me was a legend about the two hills on either side of the lake, he said there was a boy and girl who basically were in love but it was forbidden by their families so Coipre Mac Cormac, the King of Leinster turned them both into mountains and those are the hills on either side of the lake!" Fidelma looked around her excitedly, but the fairies didn't seem to be sharing her excitement, if anything they looked confused. Fairy Eimear again was the first to speak "Eh Fidelma, we don't get it, how can that help you solve the riddle?" Fidelma gasped "Oh sorry" she exclaimed, her hand flying to her mouth "I forgot to tell you the best part, apparently for a while those hills were known as. . ." Fidelma paused for effect "The man from the North and the woman from the South!" There was silence for a moment before Fairy Áine jumped up, ran around to Fidelma and threw her arms around her; the rest of the fairies began to cheer. Fidelma was delighted, it was a great feeling, tears sprang to her eyes as she imagined telling King Lír. Fairy Áine clapped her hands suddenly "Ok fairies calm down, we still have plenty of work to do." The room quietened down as everyone sat back down in their seats and Fairy Áine addressed Fidelma "Right Fidelma, we know now the root of the riddle, but how do we solve it, have you any ideas? I do not think our magic could change them back from mountains." Fidelma just smiled at Fairy Áine and took a moment before she spoke "A bridge" she said simply. The noise grew in the room as the fairies discussed this excitedly. After a moment Fairy Áine stood up "Fairy

Caoimhe" she called "We will have more tea please and some of your lovely cake to celebrate." There were cheers from the other fairies and pats on the back and hugs for Fidelma. "Tomorrow" said Fairy Áine "We shall go see King Lír and give him this good news!"

Chapter 28

Fidelmas alarm went off for the second time, and for the second time she pressed the snooze button, no sooner had she done it though and her Mother walked into her room once again opening the curtains "Come on Fidelma!

Rise and shine, breakfast finishes in an hour so get showered and packed and we'll head down to the restaurant." Fidelma groaned "Yes Mam."

Fidelma sat in the back of her parents car on the way home listening to her Fathers choice in music, she took her phone out and began flicking through the photos she had taken over the weekend, she felt a bit sad leaving Lake Derravaragh, then she came to the photo that she had sent to Aaron and she remembered he was home from his cousins, that made her smile, she decided she would call straight over to his house when she got home, she couldn't wait to see him.

******

Mr. Doyle pulled up outside their house "Home sweet home" he announced as he turned off the ignition. As they got out of the car Fidelma gave her Dad a hug "Thanks Da" she said "I had a great weekend!" Mr. Doyle hugged his daughter tight "You're welcome Fidelma, sure myself and your Mam enjoyed it too, it was great to get away." He replied as he opened the boot. "Dad" ventured Fidelma "Would you mind taking my bag in for me please while I call in to see Aaron?" Mr. Doyle smiled "Go on" he said.

Fidelma knocked on her neighbours front door, after a moment it was opened by Aarons Mother "Ah Fidelma" she said when she seen her "Come in love, Aaron will be delighted to see ye, it'll cheer him up." Fidelma followed her into the sitting room frowning "Cheer him up?" she asked "Why what's wrong with him?" Fidelma stopped at the sitting room door, Aaron was lying on the couch, he had a bandage around his head, a patch over his eye and his arms and hands were covered in dressings. "Ahoy matey!"

said Aaron jokingly. Fidelma was speechless though, she just stood staring at him, Aarons Mother broke the silence "Go on and sit down Fidelma love, I'll make some tea" and out she went to the kitchen. Aaron pulled his knees up to make room for Fidelma and she sat down on the couch "Aaron" she said, "What the heck happened to ye?" Aaron shook his head "Fidelma, you wouldn't believe me if I told ye" Fidelma stared at him "Try me" she replied. Aaron sighed "Yesterday" he started "I was coming back from the shop on my bike when all of a sudden I got whacked in the head, by a bird!" Fidelma swallowed hard, her heart was pounding "A bird?" she asked. Aaron looked at her "A bird Fidelma, like a crow or something I'm not sure, it looked like a crow but it was much bigger, it just kept coming at me squawking and pecking me, knocked me off my bike" Fidelmas hand flew to her mouth, Aaron continued "It was awful Fidelma, it was like something out of a horror movie, it was clawing at me with its claws and pecking me, I was trying to protect my head so my arms got destroyed, a man in a van pulled over and jumped out with a big stick and whacked it away, brought me to the hospital, he was sound" Fidelma just sat gaping at

Aaron "Your eye!" was all she could manage, Aaron lifted his hand to feel the patch "Yeah" he said "It pecked me in the eye, the Doctors said I was very lucky not to lose it, I've to keep the patch on for six weeks though." It was too much, Fidelma burst into tears, Aaron sat up on the couch quickly "What Fidelma? What's wrong?" Fidelma flung her arms around her best friend and sobbed "Hey" said Aaron soothingly, patting at her back "It's ok, I'm grand, I'll live" They sat like that for a minute until they were interrupted by Aarons Mother "Here you are now kiddos, I've some chocolate biccies for ye too" she sat the tray down on the coffee table in the middle of the room, she was shocked when she turned around and seen Aaron comforting a crying Fidelma "Ah love" she sat on the edge of the couch and rubbed Fidelmas back "What's wrong with you?" Fidelma tried to gather herself; she was mortified to have broken down like that. "I'm sorry Mrs. Murphy" she sniffled "I don't know what came over me there, I think it was the shock of seeing Aaron so badly hurt." Aaron leaned forward and picked up the two mugs of tea, handing one to Fidelma. "You're alright love" said Mrs. Murphy "Sure I was the same wasn't I Aaron?" Aaron nodded with a mouthful of chocolate biscuit, his Mother continued "I couldn't believe it when I got the phone call, I was imagining all sorts, and imagine my shock when he told me a bird done it! If it wasn't for the man in the van backing up his story I wouldn't have believed him, but it *was* a bird Fidelma, a crow or something!" Fidelma nodded, she wondered briefly whether or not to keep quiet about her ordeal with the bird but then decided both Mothers would be chatting and it would come out then. "Oh don't worry Mrs. Murphy, I believe him, I got attacked myself last week" she showed them the scars on her hands "it was a raven, must be a rogue one." Mrs. Murphy's face was priceless, Fidelma felt sorry for her "You're joking me?" she exclaimed "You're telling me the same bird done the same thing to you?" Fidelma smiled wryly "Well not the same exactly Mrs. Murphy, poor Aaron came off a lot worse than me but yeah it did come at me." Mrs. Murphy shook her head and tutted "I'll speak to your Mam" she declared "We'll go see the local councillor about getting rid of that bird." Fidelma and Aaron looked at each other and smiled.

That evening Fidelma was once again sitting eagerly awaiting the arrival of her Fairy friend, she had spent a couple of hours catching up with Aaron and although she enjoyed it she found it very hard to keep her anger buried, she knew what this was, Fairy Áine had told her, Aoife was sending her a warning.

Fairy Áine arrived as usual and took Fidelma to An Crann darach Sean. Once seated at the table she was greeted by Fairy Caoimhe and Fairy Eimear, "I've got Dilís ready for the trip to King Lír" said Fairy Caoimhe, Fidelma smiled at the fairy. "And I've got your travel clothes ready and some food packed" said Fairy Eimear.

Fidelma turned to the little curly haired Fairy "Fairy Eimear can you make sure my quiver is full please? I don't want to run out of arrows." Fairy Eimear nodded "Of course Fidelma." The three fairies exchanged looks, Fairy Áine spoke "Fidelma" she said "You have a strange look in your eye, what is it?" Fidelma turned to the Fairy Queen "We might know how to break the spell Fairy Áine but believe me this is far from over." Fairy Áine sat down beside Fidelma, she took her hands in hers "Tell me Fidelma." Fidelma blinked back tears, tears of sadness, tears of frustration, tears of anger "You were right, Aoife was up to something, she attacked my friend Aaron, my best friend in the whole world, she attacked him, he almost lost his eye." Fairy Áine stared at Fidelma, she could tell she was hurting; Fairy Caoimhe scurried about getting some tea. "Fidelma" said Fairy Áine gently "We are your family, we are here for you, tell us what you want us to do." Fidelma smiled at her friend and shook her head "No Fairy Áine I know that, but this is between myself and Aoife, she has declared war, and war she is going to get. I will save the children of Lír and I will take down Aoife." Fairy Áine looked at the other two fairies worryingly, Fidelma seemed to be in a trance her anger was having such an effect on her. Fairy Áine decided to take control of the situation, the trip to King Lír would have to wait. "Fairy Eimear" she spoke in her commanding voice "Fetch Cailte Mac Ronaín please" Fairy Eimear bowed to her Queen and scurried away "Fairy Caoimhe" continued Fairy Áine "Can you please send for Fairy Gittan and Fairy Pirkko please?" Fairy Caoimhe bowed and disappeared from the room. Fidelma looked up at Fairy Áine "What are you doing?" she asked. Fairy Áine sat back down beside her friend "Fidelma, I know you feel the need to do this on your own; I know that this has become personal for you, and that is fine, but you will need some help." Fairy Caoimhe re-entered the room accompanied by two male fairies, Fairy Áine stood up to introduce them. "Fidelma" she said "meet my two most powerful and strong fairies, Fairy Gittan and Fairy Pirkko" Fidelma stood up and shook the fairies hands, Fairy Áine turned to the two fairies "Boys, as you know Aoife was turned into a Demon of the air, she has attacked Fidelma in her world and now has attacked one of Fidelmas loved ones, she will do anything to prevent Fidelma from saving Lírs children, she must be stopped! We will set off to see King Lír once we have spoken with Cailte Mac Ronaín, you two will accompany us, go and get yourselves ready." The two fairies bowed to their Queen "Oh" she continued "and bring your weapons." Fidelma watched as Fairy Áine paced up and down, after a couple of minutes she turned to Fairy Caoimhe "Fairy Caoimhe, fetch Fennen please?" Fairy Caoimhe was standing at the stove stirring a cauldron of what smelled to Fidelma like porridge, she stopped at Fairy Áines request and turned to face her Queen "Fennen?" she asked sceptically, Fairy Áine replied "Yes Fairy Caoimhe, Fennan, fetch her for me." Fairy Caoimhe left the room and Fairy Áine sat down beside Fidelma again. "Who is Fennan?" asked Fidelma. "Fennen is my sister Fidelma" answered Fairy Áine "She does not live with us, she is what we call a warrior fairy, she is also powerful and strong but also extremely wise, she will be beneficial on our journey." Fidelma was taken aback, Fairy Áine had a sister? "How come she doesn't live here?" she asked. Fairy Áine closed her eyes "It pains me to say this Fidelma, but we had a falling out many years ago" Fidelma touched the Fairies hand "Oh I'm so sorry" she offered. "Oh it's fine" smiled Fairy Áine "It was a long time ago and we have since made up but Fennen chose to still live outside of An Crann darach Sean." "I see" said Fidelma, although she didn't, she wondered what could have gone on between Fairy Áine and her sister to cause such a drift, but she put it from her mind for the moment, right now she had more pressing dilemmas.

Fidelma was about to ask Fairy Áine when they would be leaving when Cailte Mac Ronaín entered the room. "Fairy Áine" he said "You sent for me?" Fidelma noticed Fairy Áine straighten her stance when Cailte walked in, she seemed to stand taller "Caitle it is good of you to come" she started "Fidelma has solved the riddle of the spell put on the children of Lír" Caitle Mac Ronaín looked over at Fidelma "That's great news Fidelma" he said smiling broadly "Well done!" Fairy Áine waved her hand interrupting him "Yes but that is not it Cailte, Aoife is out to get Fidelma, she has already attacked Fidelma in her world and now has attacked one of Fidelmas loved ones, she will stop at nothing to prevent Fidelma saving the Kings children, she has made it personal, I am in no doubt that we will encounter her on our way to see King Lír today."

Fidelma stood up at that point "But I am not afraid of her" she announced "I will not let her intimidate me like this; I want to take her down once and for all." Fairy Áine smiled at Fidelmas enthusiasm. "Yes" she said "but Fidelma cannot do this on her own, as I am sure Aoife will not be on *her* own." The two watched Cailte Mac Ronaín as he nodded before speaking "Alright, we will prepare for war so." Fidelma looked at Fairy Áine who smiled and nodded at her happily before turning to Caitle Mac Ronaín "Thank you Cailte, thank you."

Fairy Eimear came back into the room "Tea?" she asked to nobody in particular but everyone answered yes. Cailte Mac Ronaín addressed Fairy Áine "So tell me, have you a plan? Who have you got?" "Not a plan as such" replied Fairy Áine "I have sent Fairy Gittan and Fairy Pirkko to prepare to come with us." Cailte Mac Ronaín nodded his head in approval "Good, good" he said "Anyone else?" Fairy Áine looked away as she answered "eh Fennen." Fidelma watched with curiosity as she seen Cailte Mac Ronaíns expression change, was he surprised? Definitely. But was there something else going on? Maybe. "Fennen?" he asked. Fairy Áine turned to look him square in the eye "Yes Caitle, Fennen, my sister, is that alright with you?" They held each other's gaze for what seemed like ages but was probably no more than a few seconds. Fidelma could feel the tension fizzle in the room, she looked from one to the other before Cailte broke the awkward silence "Yes" he said, still holding Fairy Áines gaze "That is fine with me." Fairy Eimear broke their gaze by walking between them with the tea pot "Tea is ready" she announced before setting up cups on the table and pouring the tea. Cailte Mac Ronaín took a seat at the table "Right" he said "What we have got so far is good, but Aoife is not the only air demon, she will most likely have others with her if she attacks" he turned to look at Fidelma "and believe me Fidelma, attack she will." Fidelma nodded at him "I will be ready for her Cailte." "I believe you will" he said "but if she has an army of air demons, you too are going to need an army. "And I will" said Fidelma "I will have Fairies Pirkko and Gittan as well as Fairy Áine and Fennan." Cailte Mac Ronaín took a sip from his tea before replying "Yes Fidelma and that is good, but it is not enough, I will meet you at the edge of Leprechauns Forest." Fidelma interrupted him "Wait, leprechauns?" she looked from Cailte to Fairy Áine, eyebrows raised. "Really Fidelma?" asked Fairy Áine "You have been spending your time with fairies, learned how to speak with animals, seen children turned into swans and your questioning the existence of leprechauns? This really is not the time!" Fidelma looked contrite "Sorry Fairy Áine, sorry Cailte, please carry on." Cailte cleared his throat before continuing "I will meet you at the edge of the forest, I will have a group from the Fianna with me." Fidelma interrupted again. "I'm sorry, the Fianna?" she asked. "Yes" replied

Cailte "they are my uncles warriors, please Fidelma you can ask questions later, we really do not have any time to waste." Fidelma nodded and Cailte continued "I will go now, you will have time to get something to eat, I presume that is porridge I smell? Fill up; you're going to need your strength." And with that he stood up, nodded and made his way out the door.

"Right" declared Fairy Áine "Fairy Eimear can you dish out some porridge please? Make sure and give extra helpings, like Cailte said we are going to need our strength." Fairy Eimear got busy preparing the bowls of porridge for the team about to head out to see King Lír and possibly fight in a war on the way. Fairies Pirkko and Gittan made their way in and took their seats at the table, just as Fairy Eimear was dishing out the porridge Fairy Caoimhe came in, followed by another fairy whom Fidelma guessed was Fairy Fennan. She was quite muscular for such a petite fairy she had thick auburn hair running down her back in two thick braids, on her arms were two wide bronze bracelets like the ones Cailte wore and she had a piece of leather tied around her forehead, across her body was a thick strap which Fidelma soon realised was holding a quiver similar to hers with bows and arrow. Fairy Fennan stood in the doorway for a moment taking in the scene, Fairy Áine had been helping at the stove, she stopped what she was doing and turned around, the two sisters locked eyes, there was silence, everyone was watching when suddenly Fairy Fennan bolted towards her sister and threw her arms around her, the two fairies hugged and everyone else carried on. "Thank you for coming at such short notice Fennan" said Fairy Áine. Fairy Fennan held her sister by the arm "You are the Queen, but you are also my sister." Fairy Áine smiled, she seemed relieved. "Sit" Fairy Áine gestured to the table where a place was set for Fairy Fennan "have some porridge before we set off." Fairy Fennan took her seat, she looked over at Fidelma "You must be Fidelma" she smiled. "Yes" replied Fidelma "It's lovely to meet you." Fairy Áine took her seat. "Fennan, Fidelma is our new Protector, has Fairy Caoimhe filled you in on the situation?" "She has" answered Fairy Fennan as she began tucking into her porridge "and I have to say, you are going to need help, a proper army, I spotted Aoife two days ago and she was not alone, she had, I would say ten or twelve air demons with her and you could tell she was in charge, she was twice the size of any of the others. Have you considered getting some help?" Fairy Áine looked at her sister; Fidelma could sense tension again, what was going on? She wondered. "I have" said Fairy Áine "Cailte is going to help us." Fairy Finnans spoon stopped mid-way to her mouth, just for a second "Good" she replied "and the Fianna?" Fairy Áine looked relieved, "Yes" she said to her sister "and the Fianna, they are going to meet us at the edge of Leprechauns forest" Fairy Fennan nodded "Good idea." And that was it, they continued to eat in silence, each lost in their own thoughts.

Chapter 29

It was time for them to leave, Fidelma wasn't sure how the others were feeling, she wondered if they were nervous, she had butterflies in her stomach but it was not nerves, it was something else, something she could not put her finger on, excitement? Maybe.

Fidelma made her way over to Dilís who was ready for the trip. *"Hey boy"* she spoke to him as she rubbed his neck

"Today we're going to see King Lír but we're pretty sure Aoife will attack us en route, I know you have my back, but today more than ever I'm counting on you Dilís" Dilís nuzzled his nose against Fidelmas hand *"You can always count on me Fidelma, I promise to never let you down, if Aoife wants to get you, she will have to come through me first!"* Fidelma smiled and kissed her horse on his long nose *"Thanks boy."* She hoisted herself up on Dilís and made her way back towards the Oak tree where the fairies were waiting for her. Fairy Caoimhe had prepared Dilís well, across his back was a double sided satchel, one side

contained food and drink while the other side had little strap in seats, similar to the one Fidelma wore on her shoulder. Fairies Pirkko, Gittan and Fennan flew up into these seats and strapped themselves in, once they were secure Fairy Áine fluttered up and strapped herself in on Fidelmas shoulder, she reached over and placed her hand gently on Fidelmas cheek "Are you ready?" Fidelma smiled back at her friend "As I'll ever be" she then said to Dilís and the other fairies "Ok friends, this is it, stay safe everyone, let's go Dilís." And with that they were on their way.

They were travelling for about twenty minutes and so far all was well, Fairy Áine was giving Fidelma directions and Fidelma was then directing Dilís, they were now coming to the edge of Leprechaun forest, Fidelma felt her heartbeat quicken, not only was there no sign of the Fianna but there was no sign of Cailte Mac Ronaín either "They're not here!" Fidelma said to Fairy Áine in a panic "Why aren't they here?" "It's ok" soothed Fairy Áine "Just head to the very edge of the forest, trust me, and trust Cailte." Dilís trotted slowly towards the edge of the forest, when he came to a stop, he let out a loud neigh, except of course Fidelma heard it differently *"Team Fidelma is here!"* Fidelma smiled to herself, she liked the sound of that. Within a few seconds a group of 15 soldiers on horseback arrived from the depths of the forest, they were draped in dark green cloaks and were wearing strange masks and helmets that seemed to be made from metal and they each bore a shield and spear. A shiver ran down Fidelmas spine, she was impressed, the Fianna arranged themselves in front of Dilís in a straight line before Cailte Mac Ronaín emerged from the forest. Fidelma stared at him; he looked every bit the warrior as he brought his horse to a stop between Dilís and the Fianna. "Are you ready to do this Fidelma?" he asked. Fidelma swallowed hard "I'm ready!" she replied with conviction. Cailte Mac Ronaín looked around him as he spoke, his loud voice booming "Today we will take on evil in the form of air demons, in particular the evil Aoife, nobody stops until we have taken her down. Understood?" "Tá!" shouted the Fianna in unison. "Men! Fidelmas life and that of the fairies are your priority today, not your own lives and not mine. Do not forget that!" Fidelma raised her eyebrows muttering "Seriously?" but nobody heard her over the roar of the Fianna as they began shaking their spears in the air. "Onward!" roared Cailte.

They travelled at a moderate speed, Fidelma and Dilís flanked by the Fianna on both sides, with Cailte riding right beside them. After a few minutes Dilís spoke *"She's near Fidelma!"* Fidelma jolted *"Are you sure Dilís?"* she asked *"I don't see her"* Dilís nodded his head *"I can sense her, she's not too far up ahead"* Fidelma looked at Cailte who nodded to her "Ok men" he said "Be ready, Aoife could be in the near distance and it is likely she will have the other air demons with her." Fidelma looked either side of her as the soldiers lifted their spears at the ready, she reached over her right shoulder with her left hand and took out her bow, she reached over again and lifted as many arrows as her hand could hold. "Come on Aoife" she muttered "This is it!" As they went on further, suddenly Fidelma could see something in the distance, something black, she was guessing it was Aoife, as they got closer, she could make out the creature better. Having last seen Aoife on her Wedding day Fidelma could only imagine her rage at being turned into such an ugly beast, she looked like a cross between a giant raven and a dragon, Fidelma realised that if she had been faced with this creature a few weeks ago she probably would have passed out with fright, but no, Fidelma was determined to take Aoife down now and she felt herself bristling with anticipation at the thought of what was about to break out.

They came to a halt about 10 feet away from the wicked Aoife. Aoife spoke in her loud screechy voice "You think you are so clever Fidelma" she screamed scathingly "But I too have an army!" With that she stretched out her enormous black wings and as she did the sky darkened as more air demons appeared through the clouds, Cailte put his hands out at either side of him, signalling his army to stay put. There were ten air demons landing five either side of their leader, Fidelma looked from one to the other, she wasn't sure what she expected but it certainly wasn't what was in front of her, each of the demons were different, all ugly looking dragons but all with different shaped heads and different colour skin, some had spikes along their backs, some had horns on their head, they were pretty scary looking, but still Fidelma had no fear, she was ready. She spoke out to Aoife "Your time is up Aoife; your wickedness will destroy you in the end!" Aoife let out a screech that actually hurt Fidelmas ears "I will end you Fidelma! I. Will. End. You!" and with that she raised her wings in the air, as she did Cailte shouted to his men "Ready!" Fidelma adjusted her bow and arrow and shouted to her fairies "This is it friends, be safe!"

"ATTACK!" Screeched Aoife as she lifted off the ground followed by her army of demons. Fidelma took aim at Aoife as she flew towards her, she managed to let off 2 arrows in succession, one of which caught Aoife at the tip of her wing, not enough to do damage and certainly not enough to bring her down. The 3 Fairies Pirkko, Gittan and Fenan had undone their straps and were now flying towards Aoife. The Fianna soldiers were fighting off the smaller air demons with their spears and shields, so far two demons were down, possibly dead.

Aoife was heading for Fidelma when the three fairies reached her, they flew in front of her, spinning in a vertical line at high-speed causing a mini tornado effect, it seemed to stop Aoife mid-flight, her wings flapping in a panic to try and move forward when she simply took a deep breath and blew out a blast of air which knocked the mini tornado and the fairies to the ground. In the meantime Fidelma managed to get two more arrows fired, both landing in Aoifes tail which caused her to cry out. As Aoife again began to decent towards her nemesis, Fidelma was about to load her bow with the arrow she hoped would reach Aoife and take her down when another air demon dropped beside them knocking her slightly that she dropped her arrows, she screamed to her horse *"Dilís!"* But Dilís was already reacting, taking to a gallop to get out of the way of the descending Aoife *"I've got you*

Fidelma!" he answered. Aoife landed on the spot where Dilís had stood seconds before. Fidelma quickly retrieved another set of arrows from her quiver as Dilís turned around again towards Aoife. *"good boy Dilís"* said Fidelma as she reloaded her bow, Aoife was coming straight at her, Fidelma released her arrow just as Aoife was 5 feet from her, she caught her straight in the neck, bringing Aoife down, Fidelma was about to cheer except because of the size of Aoife she turned as she fell in agony, her left wing swiping at Fidelma, Dilís couldn't get out of the way in time, it happened so fast. Fidelma fell to the ground just as Aoife did. Fairy Áine was screaming in Fidelmas ear as she watched Aoife groan but get back to her feet "Get up Fidelma! Get up!" Fidelma shook her head and got to her feet, she reached up to her shoulder and quickly undid Fairy Áines strap "Go to Dilís" she said to her fairy friend, Fairy Áine flew up to Fidelmas face "What? Fidelma no, you need to get back on Dilís, come on!" But Fidelma didn't even look at her; her eyes were locked with the evil Aoifes "Go!" She shouted at Fairy Áine, the fairy quickly flew to Dilís and clung to his mane "What is she doing Dilís? Help her!" she screamed helplessly.

But Dilís spoke gently to Fidelma *"Go Fidelma, I've got your back!"* Fidelma had a quick look around her, the Fianna were still fighting, a couple were on the ground nursing minor injuries, only three of four air demons were left, Fidelma spotted a soldier down on the ground between her and Aoife, she began to walk forward "It's just me and you now Aoife, just me and you" It all happened so quick, Fidelma started to run towards the giant demon, running past the fallen soldier she whipped his spare spear from its holder on his back and charged, Aoife stood up on her back legs, spread her wings out and screeched "I will end you Fidelma" Her words ringing out in a painful roar as Fidelma launched the spear into her heart, her wails of agony brought everyone to a stop. Fidelma stood and watched as Aoife seemed to fall in slow motion, Fidelma was glued to the spot, completely breathless as she waited. Aoife was down and she was not moving. Cailte Mac Ronaín came over and put his hand on Fidelmas shoulder as he walked past to check the fallen demon, he put his boot under her head and moved it slightly, then bent down to put his ear to her chest, there was silence as everyone waited, he turned and looked around him for a couple of seconds before speaking "She is dead!" he announced, still silence, then Fidelma's face broke into a smile and she began laughing, a relieved laugh. Cailte Mac Ronaín walked over and put his arms around her "Well done Fidelma, you did well" Fidelma smiled up at him "I cannot thank you enough for your help Cailte, I will be eternally grateful" she replied and with that she turned around to see Dilís staring at her with her four fairy companions standing on his head, the Fianna all watching her, some standing some sitting but all alive and around them were scattered the bodies of ten air demons. Fidelma smiled, thrust her bow in the air and cheered, everyone joined in, she was sure their cheers could be heard throughout the land.

Chapter 30

They were all sitting by a stream not too far from where their battle had taken place less than an hour ago, Fairy Áine and Fairy Fennan were tending to a couple of the soldiers wounds, they weren't life threatening, just cuts. Fidelma was sitting on the grass, her long limbs stretched out in the sunshine; Cailte Mac Ronaín came over and sat down beside her. "How are you feeling?" he asked. Fidelma thought for a moment, how *was* she feeling? She wasn't too sure, happy? Yes of course and relieved that her loved ones were no longer in danger, but there was something else, she turned to look at Cailte Mac Ronaín, shielding her eyes from the strong sun "I'm not sure" she answered "I'm happy, you know? Glad, relieved, but there's something else, it's in the pit of my stomach." Cailte Mac Ronaín smiled at her "That's pride Fidelma." Fidelma looked at him, her eyebrows raised "Pride?" she asked unsure. "Pride" answered the warrior "And pride is exactly what you should be feeling Fidelma, you have just brought down an extremely evil air demon, believe it or not, you have saved lives, and on top of that you are on your way to save King Lírs children, that is pretty special. You have only been doing this job for a short time" He stood up "You are going to make a great Protector Fidelma" Cailte Mac Ronaín touched her shoulder again before making his way over to check on his men. Fidelma sat for a moment letting his words sink in when all of a sudden she felt her eyes well up, she fought hard to keep those tears from falling but one managed to escape and drop from her eye, she quickly wiped it away with the back of her hand hoping nobody had seen, no sooner had she done so though and Fairy Áine fluttered over landing on her lap. "Oh no you don't mo chara" she said wagging her finger, Fidelma laughed as another tear escaped, "I'm not crying" she said, Fairy Áine raised her eyebrows, Fidelma giggled "I'm just overwhelmed by it all, I actually can't believe what just happened." Fairy Áine smiled affectionately at her friend "Of course you are overwhelmed, what you just did is huge." She flew up and kissed Fidelma on the cheek before coming back down to rest on her lap again. Fairy Fennan joined them, sitting beside Fairy Áine she spoke to Fidelma "So Fidelma, our new Protector, you have just proved to be worth your weight in gold, we are very lucky to have you, I hope we can be friends too." Fidelma looked at Fairy Áine questioningly, the Fairy Queen smiled and nodded. "Thank you" said Fidelma "I am honoured to have you all as my friends." Fairy Fennan stood up "Right I am going to re fill my canteen." Fairy Áine sat smiling at Fidelma, "What?" asked Fidelma her cheeks turning pink. "Fidelma the Warrior" said Fairy Áine, "it has a good ring to it."

Cailte Mac Ronaín walked back over to Fidelma "Right Fidelma, my men are ready to get going now, unless you need us for anything else?" Fidelma stood up shaking her head "No" she replied "I think the danger is gone now" she extended her hand for Cailte to take "I cannot thank you enough for your help." she said. Cailte took her hand and gave it a good strong shake "Anytime Fidelma, it was fun" he answered giving her a wink before gathering his men.

Fidelma walked over to Dilís who was still drinking water from the stream *"you ok to keep going now boy?"* she asked him. Dilís lifted his head up from the water *"Of course Fidelma, are you ok?"* Fidelma smiled as she patted her loyal horse on the side of his neck *"I'm fine Dilís, I'm absolutely fine."* *"Good"* replied Dilís *"In case I forget to tell you when we get home, I am incredibly proud of you, you done well kid"* Fidelma was taken aback but also chuffed with this huge compliment, she smiled as she planted a kiss on the length of Dilís nose *"Thank you Dilís, you didn't do so bad yourself."* Fidelma turned around "Ok friends" she said to the fairies "time to get going." She hoisted herself up onto Dilís, while the fairies strapped themselves in she watched as Cailte Mac Ronaín and the Fianna went to head off in the opposite direction when she thought of something.

"Cailte!" Fidelma called out. Cailte Mac Ronaín turned his horse around and made his way over to her "Fidelma? Is everything alright?" he asked when he reached her. "I just had a thought" replied Fidelma "King Lír is going to need some help to build a bridge, is that something you think your men would be willing to do?" Cailte gave Fidelma one of his charming smiles "My uncle's men Fidelma, but yes, I am quite sure that is something they would be willing to do" He looked at Fairy Áine on Fidelmas shoulder "Fairy Áine maybe you can let me know the details in the next day or so?" Fairy Áine nodded in reply "Of course Cailte, we will be in touch, thank you." And with that Cailte Mac Ronaín and the Fianna were gone.

Chapter 31

The little group finally arrived at King Lírs. Fidelma led Dilís over to graze and she walked up to the door, with the four fairies fluttering along beside her. The two knights simply bowed their head and stood aside to let them pass. Fidelma found herself in the dark hallway again, as she walked towards the door in front of her she thought back to the last time she was here, she remembers feeling nervous and unsure of herself, of what to expect, of how to speak to the King in such tragic circumstances. She was feeling different this time, she walked in confidence down the long hallway, she felt happy, so happy to be able to give King Lír the good news, and yes, she was also very proud of herself, she had come a long way since putting that little key into the treasure chest.

Fidelma reached the heavy wooden door and she knocked hard, once again she heard the deep booming voice from the other side call out "Come in!" Fidelma opened the door and entered the big room, King Lír was standing by the table, "Come come, sit down" he gestured to a seat, "I'm just preparing to head to the lake." Fidelma sat down as the fairies sat themselves on the table, King Lír called out to his trusty servant before sitting down "Ardeen, can you bring tea please? Fidelma and four fairies!" He sat himself down and addressed his guest. "So Fidelma, to what do I owe the pleasure? Do you have any news for me?" Fidelma looked at her fairy friends, their faces were beaming, she couldn't believe she was actually about to deliver the news King Lír had being praying for, she turned to the King "Yes King Lír" she said smiling "I have news, I have some very good news." King Lír looked at her eagerly, Fidelma closed her eyes and took a deep breath, she wanted to remember this moment. "I won't bore you with the details today but, I have worked out the riddle of Aoifes spell" Fidelma watched as the Kings expression changed, it softened as she spoke "and not only have I worked it out but I know how to solve it, all we need to do is build a bridge across the lake, to connect the two mountains and that will be it, the spell should be broken!" She waited, she waited for King Lír to start cheering, but he just sat there silently, still she waited, searching his face for clues as to how he was feeling when she noticed his eyes glistening, then slowly welling up, Fidelma and the fairies watched as this big strong King covered his face with his hands and sobbed like a baby. It was a much more powerful reaction than Fidelma could have expected, it was very emotional to watch, but watch they did, they just sat watching him, mesmerized, not sure what to do. Suddenly the door opened and in walked Ardeen carrying a tray of tea and bread, when she seen King Lír sitting there crying she ran over to him, dumping the tray loudly on the table "Oh King Lír" she cried, her hands going to her mouth "Whatever is it? Not the children! Please don't tell me it's the children?" Before anyone else could answer, King Lír jumped up from his seat, he threw his arms around the startled servant, hugging her tightly, he then held her by the shoulders at arms length "My children have been saved Ardeen! My children have been saved!" he then picked Ardeen up and began spinning her around cheering "Whoooowhoooo!" Ardeen was getting giddy "What? Oh King Lír is it true?" King Lír turned to Fidelma and the fairies "Well? Tell the woman!" he said happily. Fidelma and the fairies nodded excitedly "Yes" said Fidelma, feeling her own eyes moisten now "It's true Ardeen, it's true!" Ardeen began to jump up and down with pure joy. Fidelma looked at Fairy Áine "I think this is the greatest moement of my life" she exclaimed. Fairy Áine walked over and touched her friends hand "Hold that thought Fidelma, I think you will be experiencing greater joy when the spell is actually broken."

The pair smiled at each other. Fidelma looked at Fairies Gittan, Pirkko and Fennan, they were hugging and wiping tears from their eyes, everyone was feeling the emotion.

Fidelma poured herself some tea and cleared her throat. "So King Lír" The King turned to look at Fidelma "we'll just discuss some details and then we can head to the lake." King Lír took his seat again "Yes of course Fidelma, go ahead." Fairy Áine and the other three fairies took their seats again too, Ardeen stood behind the Kings seat, her hands clutched together at her chest as she listened to what

Fidelma had to say. "I am confident the spell will be broken" started Fidelma "first though, a bridge needs to be built to connect the south mountain to the north mountain, that's the important part, that they're reconnected." King Lír was nodding, "Now, I have asked Cailte Mac Ronaín for his help and he has agreed to have the men from the Fianna build the bridge." King Lír was impressed "That is good, that is very good" he said. "We'll send word to let you know when the bridge will be started once the details have been finalised" continued Fidelma "Until then, you'll need to be patient, I know you want the children back right now but it's not going to happen over night, I'm not sure how long it will take for the bridge to be built, but we'll get there. The other thing is" Fidelma paused as she turned to Fairy Áine, she got the nod from her friend to go ahead, so she continued "So I have another piece of news for you" Fidelma was actually nervous, suddenly she didn't feel as confident as she felt earlier or as proud of killing Aoife the wicked air demon, the wife of King Lír! She hesitated, Fairy Áine stood up and walked over to Fidelma "The thing is King Lír" said Fairy Áine "Fidelma has been through a tough time of late,

Aoife has been out to get her" King Lír interrupted "Yes I feared that would happen" Fairy Áine nodded "yes" she began again "so not only was it unsafe for her here but Aoife followed her to the New World." Before Fairy Áine continued King Lír had jumped up banging his fist on the table "That is it!" he roared, making poor Ardeen leap with fright behind him, he turned to her "Ardeen" he said, his voice shaking with rage "send for my guards, it is high time Aoife was dealt with" Fidelma stood up now too, she gently put her hand on the Kings arm "Actually King Lír" he turned to face her as she shook her head "You don't need to call your guards, Aoife is dead." The King hung his head, there was silence. Fidelma looked at the fairies, Fairy Áine shrugged her shoulders, she looked back at the King "I'm sorry" Fidelma whispered, slowly the King raised his head to look at her "Sorry?" he asked "Why are *you* sorry Fidelma?" Fidelma was sure she could hear her heart pounding; she wondered if anyone else in the room could hear it. Fidelma spoke in a small voice "It was I who killed her!" King Lír peered at her "You?" he asked quietly. "Me." Whispered Fidelma, she held her breath. King Lír suddenly threw his arms around her "Well then I owe you my deepest gratitude Fidelma". Fidelma felt her body relax with relief. Fairy Fennan spoke up "Shall we go tell the children now?" Everyone turned to look at her. "Yes" said King Lír "yes, let's go and tell the children." The fairies all smiled at each other, Fairy Áine winked at Fidelma. "Shall I ask Padraig to get your horse ready sir?" asked Ardeen, King Lír turned to his servant. "Yes" he said "yes please Ardeen."

Chapter 32

They arrived at Lake Derravaragh, as Fidelma climbed down from Dilís she took in her surroundings, it was still the same place but it looked different. She stood on the shore and looked across at the two mountains, she could just about make out the shape of two faces, and she wondered how she had never noticed it before. Fidelma could see the swans out in the middle of the lake; she put her hand up to wave to them. King Lír came over and stood beside her "Children!" he called to them "Come children, we have some news." The children arrived at the shore, they were happy to see their Father and also Fidelma. King

Lír spoke first "Children, Fidelma has something to tell you." Fidelma was shocked, she looked at King Lír, and he simply smiled and nodded his head to her. Fidelma took a deep breath; she never imagined she would be the one breaking the news to the children, she felt extremely honoured.

"Children" she began "in the next few days you will see some activity around the lake, Cailte Mac Ronaín and the Fianna will be building a bridge from one side of the lake to the other" she paused for moment, the swans looked from one to the other, she could tell they had no idea what this meant for them, she continued "children, once that bridge is finished, the spell will be broken, you will be free!" The children began shouting with joy, Fionnuala stopped though "Wait" she said "Fidelma, what about Aoife, she will never allow this to happen, I am worried for your safety" Fidelma smiled, she had a lump in her throat at the kindness of Fionnualas words, King Lír stepped forward just then and spoke "Fidelma has already taken care of that Fionnuala, your wicked stepmother is dead." The children broke into tears; King Lír got down on his knees on the wet pebbles and hugged his children. Fidelma began to back away silently, she walked over to where the fairies were waiting with Dilís "I think it's time to go home" she said.

★★★★★★

They arrived safely back at An Crann Darach Sean, Dilís had galloped at full speed the whole way back, they didn't even stop for a break, Fidelma was happy to finally see the oak tree, it felt like so long since they had left it even though it was only a few hours ago, so much had happened in such a short time. Fidelma climbed down from Dilís and the fairies all undone their seat straps, Dilís turned to Fidelma *"Fidelma you have had a busy day, go have some tea, I can make my own way over to the field."* Fidelma smiled at her faithful companion, she leaned her face against his neck and rubbed his mane *"Thank you Dilís, for everything, I'll see you tomorrow."* Dilís trotted off, Fidlema took Fairy Áines hand and they went into An Crann Darach Sean.

They were greeted straight away by an anxious looking Fairy Caoimhe followed by an equally anxious looking Fairy Eimear, "Well?" the two fairies asked in unison, Fidelma looked around at Fairies Áine, Fennan, Pirkko and Gittan, she smiled at Fairies Caoimhe and Eimear "Have we got quiet the tale for you." she said.

Chapter 33

Fidelma was back in her bedroom, she was absolutely shattered, she felt like she could sleep for a week, she slipped into her pyjamas and climbed into bed, she hadn't even the energy to go downstairs and say goodnight to her parents. Fidelma closed her eyes, after a minute she opened them again, her body was tired but her brain was racing, what a day! She thought about

Fairy Fennan, her face was the same as Fairy Áines yet they were totally different, she wondered what had gone on between them, she had so many questions, but had a feeling it had something to do with Cailte Mac Ronaín. Fidelma felt a smile spread across her face as she remembered the joy on King Lírs face and the happiness he shared with his children, she would remember those moments forever. Fidelma felt her eyes close, but as soon as they did she saw Aoife falling down in slow motion again, her eyes flew open, her heart pounding, now there was a moment she hoped did not stay with her forever.

******

The next morning Fidelma came down the stairs and headed into the kitchen. Mrs. Doyle was in there cooking a fry up. "Ah good morning sleepy head" she said to her daughter, Fidelma smiled at her Mother and took a seat at the counter. "I didn't know where you went to last night, I went up to check on you and there you were, tucked up in your bed fast asleep." Fidelma stretched and yawned "I know Mam, I was so tired, I was reading and then I just climbed into bed." Mrs. Doyle handed Fidelma a cup of tea "Must've been all that lovely fresh air" she said. Fidelma sipped at her tea "Mmm must've been." "Well you got up at the right time, I've a fry on for the four of us, it's nearly ready." Fidelma frowned "Four of us?" she asked. "Dad and Sean." replied Mrs. Doyle. "Oh" said Fidelma "Are they not in work today?" Mrs. Doyle turned to look at her daughter "Fidelma, it's a bank holiday! Are you still asleep?"

Mr. Doyle and Sean came into the kitchen just as the food was ready, Fidelma helped her mother set the table and they all sat down to eat. "I heard about Aaron" said Sean. Mr. and Mrs. Doyle looked at their son, Mrs.

Doyle turned to Fidelma "What happened to Aaorn?" she asked her, before Fidelma could answer though Sean spoke again "Got knocked off his bike, ended up in hospital." Mrs. Doyle was shocked "You're joking me, is he ok?" Fidelma smiled wryly "He's grand Mam, a few bandages but no broken bones; he has to wear an eye patch for a few weeks though." Mr. Doyle put his fork down "An eye patch?" he asked "how did he do damage to his eye if he fell off his bike?" Once again Sean got in there before Fidelma could "That's the best part Da, you won't believe what knocked him off his bike" Sean looked at his parents keeping them in suspense for a moment before continuing "Fidelmas crow!" he said nodding towards his sister. Mr. and Mrs. Doyle looked at their daughter now "Is this true Fidelma?" her mother asked. Fidlema stuck a forkful of food in her mouth before she answered, to give herself time to arrange her words in her head first "Mmmm" she started "Yeah and it was a Raven actually Sean, must be a rogue one, Mrs. Murphy is reporting it the council." Her parents were staring at her openmouthed "And what about his eye?" asked her Father. "Oh yeah" said Fidelma "It pecked at his eye, the doctors said he was very lucky not to lose it, he just needs to wear the patch for 6 weeks though." "Nice" said Sean "perfect way to start back at school, with an eyepatch" and he shook his head. "Well" said Mr. Doyle "that bird better not show up around here again or it'll be sorry." Fidelma just carried on eating.

After breakfast Fidelma went upstairs and changed into her tracksuit, she ran back down the stairs and shouted into the kitchen as she was heading out the front door "Just calling into Aaron."

Fidelma knocked on Aaron's front door, soon after it was opened by Aaron "Hey

Fidelma" he said as he stood back "come on in." They walked into the kitchen where Aaron switched on the kettle. "Great to see you up and about again Aaron" said Fidelma to her friend. "Ah I'm grand Fidelma" smiled Aaron. Fidelma watched as Aaron got two mugs from the cupboard and popped a tea bag into each of them. "So" she ventured "I went for a bit of a walk this morning, and you won't believe what I seen?" Aaron looked at her questioningly, Fidelma continued "Our raven, dead!" Aaron frowned "What? Dead? How?" Fidelma shrugged "Not sure" she said "could've been hit by a car or something, but it was definitely our raven and it was definitly dead, believe me." Aaron handed Fidelma her mug of tea "well, that's great news" he said and he clinked his mug against Fidelmas "Cheers to no more freaky raven attacks." Fidelma smiled "Yeah, cheers to that." She took a sip from her tea and thought, if only Aaron knew the half of it, she wondered how he would have reacted had he seen the actual size of the 'raven'.

Later that evening Fidelma excused herself from the sitting room where the rest of the family were watching the 'bank holiday movie'. "I'm just going upstairs to read" she announced as she stood up. "I must borrow that book after you Fidelma, you can't seem to put it down." said Mrs. Doyle to her daughter. Fidelma stopped at the sitting room door "Eh, yeah, sure." she replied. Fidelma ran up the stairs to her bedroom and sat down on her bed, Fairy Áine popped out almost immediately and as usual flew up and kissed Fidelma on the tip of her nose "How is my warrior today?" she asked smiling. Fidelma beemed at the little fairy "Oh you know, happy." Fairy Áine put out her hand "Come on!"

An Crann darach Sean was a hive of activity. Fairies were scurrying about busily; Fidelma looked around her as she walked towards the table. Fairy Caoimhe was making tea and turned when she heard Fidelma come in, she stopped what she was doing and ran over to hug Fidelma "Oh Fidelma it is so good to see you, how are you feeling?" Fidelma was taken aback by the enthusiastic greeting. "Yeah I'm good" she replied as she took a seat at the table "Happy, relieved you know?" Fairy Coimhe nodded excitedly "Of course of course" she replied "Fidelma we are all so proud of you." she squealed. Fairy Áine smiled at her fairy friend.

"So" started Fidelma "What's been happening?" "Well" said Fairy Áine "the fairies have all been very busy, Cailte was here and we went through plans for the bridge, the Fianna were collecting logs and the fairies have been making rope." Fidelma was a bit surprised that things had started moving already "Oh" she exclaimed "So they've already made a start?" Fairy Áine nodded "They've already started and it is coming along nicely, we will take you to see it but maybe tomorrow, today we thought you would like to just take it easy." Fairy Caoimhe placed a pot of tea on the table with some cups, "Have some tea" said Fairy

Áine, Fairy Caoimhe returned to the table with a plate of bread and a pot of strawberry jam, she smiled at Fidelma "Fairy Eimear made this fresh this morning." Fidelmas eyes lit up, her Granny used to make her own jam and it was delicious, she only had shop bought since her Granny passed away and it just wasn't the same. "So" said Fidelma as she slathered some jam on a piece of bread "have you seen much of Fairy Fennan since?" No sooner had Fidelma spoken when Fairy Fennan entered the room "I'm still here" she said smiling. Fidelma looked from Fairy Áine to her sister, they were both smiling like children on

Christmas morning, and it was lovely. "Wow!" said Fidelma "That's great." Fairy Áine nodded "Yes Fairy Fennan is going to stay with us for a few days to help with the rope making; it takes a lot of hands to weave grass into rope strong enough to make a bridge." "I can imagine." said Fidelma. Fairy Fennan joined them at the table and there was silence for a couple of minutes while they all enjoyed the yummy bread and jam. "I thought I'd go see Dilís and spend a bit of time with him" said Fidelma. "That sounds like a lovely idea Fidelma" said Fairy Áine.

After they had finished their tea Fidelma stood up to leave "Right I'm going to head out then." she said to nobody in particular. Fairy Caoimhe spoke up "I'll come out with you Fidelma, I'm going to see some bees about some honey." she said smiling. They said goodbye to Fairies Áine and Fennan and headed out.

Once outside the oak tree, Fidelma was back to her normal size and Fairy Caoimhe fluttered along beside her shoulder as she walked through the field towards Dilís. It was another beautiful warm sunny day in Old Ireland; Fidelma inhaled the sweet smell of the fresh grass as she walked through the field. "It must be nice" said Fairy Caoimhe "to be able to walk around without looking over your shoulder anymore." "It certainly is" said Fidelma. "Tell me, why did Fairy Áine and Fairy Fennan fall out?" Fidelma asked. She knew if she was going to find out anything it would be from Fairy Caoimhe, she was so sweet but she loved a good gossip. "Well" started Fairy Caoimhe conspiratorially "A long time ago when we were younger we were all such great friends, myself, Fairies Áine, Fennan and Eimear grew up together so as you can imagine as fairy children we got up to all sorts of mischief" said Fairy Caoimhe with a giggle. Fidelma smiled as she tried to imagine them as children. "We were also friends with non fairies, Fairy Áine had been very good friends with King Lír and Aoibh, we were also good friends with Cailte and his cousin Oisín, we used to have great fun together, we would turn the boys fairy size and play in the oak tree or swim in a stream, we were very close. But then as we got older things got complicated." Fidelma stopped walking "Let's sit here for a minute" she said to the fairy as she sat down on the soft grass "Complicated how?" Fidelma asked. "Both Fairy Áine and

Fairy Fennan fell in love with Cailte Mac Ronaín" continued Fairy Caoimhe "he was fond of them both but it was clear to me that he was in love with Fairy Áine. At first it was fine, the two sisters made a pact that neither would pursue Cailte, it was sweet really, they were putting each other first, before their own feelings." Fidelma was captivated by Fairy Caoimhes story "But then" continued Fairy Caoimhe "One night we were having a festival to mark the opening of a new fairyring, everyone was dancing and having fun when Fairy Fennan realised she couldn't find Fairy Áine so she went to look for her, she found her not far away but behind a tree with Cailte, she seen Cailte kiss her sister and declare his love for her." Fidelma was astounded "What did she do?" asked Fidelma quietly. "Well" said Fairy Caoimhe "It is no mistake that Fairy Fennan is a warrior fairy, she is strong but she is also fiery and she flew into a rage accusing her sister of breaking their pact, that night she moved out of An Crann darach Sean and never returned." Fidelma was speechless; she sat thinking about the story, such drama! She had questions though "So how long was it until they spoke again?" asked Fidelma. "King Eógabail, their father became ill and the sisters were together again for the first time in two years when they gathered at his death bed. There he told Fairy Áine that she would become Queen of the Fairies, Fairy Fennan was happy for her of course and congratulated her, but she never moved back to the Oak tree. Instead she carved out a new home for herself in another tree." Fidelma thought for a moment "What about Cailte Mac Ronaín?" she asked. "He begged Fairy Áine to marry him but she told him being Queen was too important to her and she didn't have the time to marry, however he knew it was because of the pact and he never really forgave Fairy Fennan." Fairy Caoimhe was finished her story. "Wow!" exclaimed Fidelma "I don't know what to say." "Oh" pipped Fairy Caoimhe "Please do not say anything, Fairy Áine always tells me I have too much to say." Fidelma smiled at Fairy Caoimhe, Fairy Áine was right. "Do you think Cailte Mac Ronaín is still in love with Fairy Áine?" she asked as she stood up. "Oh of course" said Fairy Caoimhe fluttering her wings "It is as clear as the sun in the sky, he would marry her tomorrow but Fairy Áine is just so stubborn." Fidelma laughed, Fairy Caoimhe was right, these little fairies knew each other better than they knew themselves.

As Fidelma made her way towards Dilís, Fairy Caoimhe headed off towards a beehive. Fidelma was still thinking about the story she had just heard. She knew there was a spark between Fairy Áine and Cailte Mac Ronaín, what a shame her fairy friend was so stubborn, a fairy wedding would be amazing she smiled.

Fidelma reached Dilís *"Hey there boy"* she called to him. *"I knew I heard footsteps"* came his reply. *"Fancy going for a walk?"* Fidelma asked the horse. Dilís stretched out his two front legs to bring his body down lower *"climb on!"* he said. Fidelma climbed on and off they went. They trotted along slowly first, chatting. *"Did you get a good rest?"* Dilís asked of Fidelma. *"I did"* she replied *"I slept for twelve hours!"* They trotted on for another bit before Dilís spoke again *"You did great yesterday kid, I was so proud of you"*. *"Thanks"* replied Fidelma *"But I knew you had my back. That gave me strength." "I will always have your back Fidelma"* said Dilís. *"But you did not need me Fidelma; you did it on your own."* Fidelma patted her horse on the side of his neck *"I'll always need you Dilís, now lets *see how fast we can go."* With that Dilís took off and they galloped off through the long grass.

Chapter 34

Fidelma was heading home with her Mother after a day out shopping for last bits and pieces for school. She couldn't believe she was back to school in just over a week, the summer went so quick since she got the treasure chest, in fact things had been so frantic the last couple of weeks that Fairy Áine gave Fidelma a few days off, she gave Fidelma strict instructions to rest up and enjoy time with her family. So that is exactly what Fidelma was doing. Shopping today with her Mother, yesterday she went for a game of crazy golf with her Dad which was great fun and the day before she went into town with her brother Sean where he treated her to lunch. As Mrs. Doyle drove her car into the driveway Aaron appeared from his house. "He must've been watching out the window for you to come home" said Mrs. Doyle smiling. Fidelma was mortified "Mam don't be ridiculous." She climbed out of the car "Hi Aaron!" she greeted her friend as she gathered up her bags. Mrs. Doyle made her way to the front door and called to them "I'll stick the kettle on!" Aaron leaned into the car to lift some of the bags "here let me help, how was the shopping trip?" Fidelma gestured to the shopping bags "What do you think?" she said giggling. "The usual so" said Aaron. They carried the bags into the house and on into the kitchen. Mrs. Doyle had the kettle on, the cups out and the tea bags in the tea pot, she busied herself getting out a packet of biscuits and putting some on a plate. "How's the eye?" Mrs. Doyle asked Aaron. "Yeah yeah it's grand thanks, I was back at the hospital yesterday and the doctor said it's healing nicely." Mrs. Doyle smiled at him "Ah that's good news." She filled the tea pot with boiling water and put it on the stove. Fidelma was looking at Aaron, he was acting strange "Is everything ok Aaron?" she asked. "What?" he seemed flustered "Oh yeah I'm grand thanks. Grand." Mrs. Doyle smiled to herself as she poured her own cup of tea "Right Fidelma" she said to her daughter "I'm going in to put my feet up and watch TV, there's tea in the pot, help yourselves." and out she went. Fidelma went to the stove and poured out two mugs of tea, she handed one to Aaron, she picked up the plate and offered it to him

"Biscuit?" she asked. Aaron put his hand up "No Fidelma, no thanks." Fidelma frowned, Aaron definitely wasn't himself. She watched him as he sipped at his tea, then he put his mug down on the counter and spoke "Fidelma do you want to come to the cinema with me this evening?" Fidelma looked at him "Yeah sure, who else is going?" Pink spots start appearing on Aarons cheeks "Eh, no one else. I meant on a date actually!" Fidelmas eyes widenend "Oh!" she exclaimed, she could feel her own cheeks turn pink "Sure, yeah that'd be lovely, thanks." Aaron smiled relieved and reached for the plate of biscuits "I'll take that biscuit" he said.

******

Later that evening Aaron and Fidelma got off the bus on their way home from the cinema. They had enjoyed the movie and gone for chips and a milkshake after. Now they were walking back home from the bus stop. "I really enjoyed tonight Aaron" said Fidelma. "Yeah me too." said Aaron smiling. The next thing Fidelma felt Aaron take her hand without saying a word, she let him hold it and they walked on companionably. When they got to their houses they stood outside Fidelmas driveway. "So" said Fidelma feeling strangely embarrassed. "So" said Aaron, equally embarrassed. "I should go in" said Fidelma. "Yeah. Ok. Cool. Eh, would you like to do this again sometime?" Fidelma beamed "I'd love to Aaron" she said. Aaron gave a nervous laugh "Great" he said, and then he leaned over and kissed Fidelma on the cheek "See you tomorrow!" Fidelmas cheeks went pink with delight "See you tomorrow!" and she walked into her house as Aaron walked to his house.

Fidelma opened the front door and let herself in. Straight away she heard her Mother "Is that you Fidelma?"

Fidelma stood in the hallway and called into her Mother in the sitting room "Yeah it's me Mam." No sooner had she said it and her Mother popped her head out of the doorway "Come in tell us all about it." Fidelma sighed as she walked into the sitting room "What?" she asked embarrassed "It was just the cinema!" Mrs. Doyle was sitting on the couch gazing up at her daughter "Fidelma" she said "It was your first date, tell me all about it." Fidelmas face reddened. "Mam!" she exclaimed. Mr. Doyle put down his newspaper "Ah leave the girl alone you're embarrassing her. Had you a good time Fidelma?" Fidelma relaxed

"Yes Dad thanks, it was lovely, I'm going up to my room." And up the stairs she ran, eager to get away from her inquisitive mother.

Fidelma sat down at her dressing table and looked at herself in her mirror, she touched her cheek where Aaron had kissed her and smiled. Fairy Áine was peering out from the treasure chest at her friend; slowly she lifted the lid and climbed out. She walked across the dressing table and stood in front of Fidelma. Fidelma jumped when she seen her "Jeez Fairy Áine you scared me!" she exclaimed putting her hand to her chest "how did you do that? How did you get out so quietly?" Fairy Áine stood looking at Fidelma for a moment "I've been here a while Fidelma, I arrived in my usual way but when you weren't here I climbed back into the chest to wait, I thought you wouldn't be long. There is something different about you mo chara, what is it?" Fidelma shrugged her shoulders embarrassed. "I've no idea" she said. Fairy Áine squinted her eyes suspiciously. Fidelma just stood up "Right are we going?" she put her hand out for Fairy Áine to take.

Chapter 35

There was an air of excitement at An Crann darach Sean and Fidelma was intrigued but Fairy Áine was clearly giving nothing away. As usual Fairy Caoimhe was preparing the tea, Fairies Gittan, Pirkko, Eimear and Fennan were sitting at the table chatting, when Fidelma walked in with Fairy Áine they stopped. "Hi" said Fidelma giving a little wave and taking a seat. "Hi Fidelma, we've missed you around here" said Fairy Eimear. "I've missed being here" said Fidelma "but I did enjoy the rest, I've had a fun few days." Fairy Áine sat down beside her "So Fidelma" she said "Have you any news for us?" Once again Fidelma felt her cheeks turn pink "No not really." Fairy Áine looked at her friend and smiled "How is your friend Aaron?" Fidelma didn't answer she just stared at Fairy Áine. The other fairies watched the two friends to see what was unfolding. "Oh come on!" squealed Fairy Áine "Spill the beans! Or whatever it is you say in New Ireland." Fidelma burst out laughing, she couldn't help it. "Ok" she started and the fairies all moved in closer to her. "Myself and Aaron went on a date tonight, we went to see a movie and then we went for some chips, and it was nice." "Just a movie and chips?" asked Fairy Áine, Fidelma giggled "He might have kissed me on the cheek!" "Woooohoooo!!" Cheered fairies Áine, Caoimhe, Eimear and Fennan. Fidelma was mortified but she laughed with her friends. Fairy Caoimhe sat the tea on the table with some mugs and Fairy Fennan poured for everyone. "Right" spoke Fairy Áine "Fidelma we are taking you on a little trip today." "Oh" said Fidelma taken aback "I wasn't expecting that, what kind of a trip?" "It is a surprise" said Fairy Fennan and the rest of the Fairies grinned at her. "We have prepared Dilís for the trip and we are all coming with you" said Fairy Caoimhe.

"Oooh" said Fidelma rubbing her hands together "Sounds exciting!"

When they had finished their tea the little group left the oak tree and headed across the field towards Dilís, Fidelma could see he had a satchel across his back like the last time except this one had extra seats for the extra fairies. *"Do you know where they're taking me?"* Fidelma asked Dilís. *"Of course."* Fidelma shook her head. She climbed up onto Dilís and the fairies all strapped themselves in, Fairy Áine strapping herself into the seat on Fidelmas shoulder and away they went. After they had been traveling for a while Dilís slowed down *"what is it boy?"* Fidelma asked him feeling naturally nervous. *"Don't worry Fidelma, there's nothing wrong I just wondered if it would be ok if we took a break for a few minutes?"* Fidelma rubbed his neck *"Oh of course Dilís, stop here if you like?"* *"Actually"* replied Dilís *"There's a stream just over there I wouldn't mind a drink?"* *"Lead the way"* said Fidelma simply.

Fidelma hopped down off Dilís and let him drink from the stream, she walked around stretching her legs and arms, the fairies were fluttering around her happily in the sunshine. Fidelma slipped off her shoes and walked to the stream, she rolled up her trousers and walked into the water, the fairies watched her for a moment before fluttering above the water and splashing it up Fidelmas legs, Fidelma giggled and bent down to flick water on them with her fingers. It was such simple fun and Fidelma thought she could spend all day here cooling down from the hot sun in this bubbly little stream. All of a sudden their laughter was interrupted by Dilís "Eh excuse me Fidelma?" Fidelma looked over at him "I'm trying to drink this water!" Fidelma held in her laugh "And?" she asked him. "And your stinky feet are in it!" Fidelma burst out laughing, she ran over and began kicking water up at Dilís *"Bad move Fidelma"* said the witty horse *"This is one war you can't win"* and he kicked hard at the water drenching Fidelma from head to toe. "Aaaaaaghh!" Screamed Fidelma laughing *"Dilís I can't believe you did that!"* She trudged through the stream onto the grass and began wringing out her top and trousers, she then lay down on the grass beside where the fairies were sitting still laughing. *"You're gonna have to wait till I'm dry now Dilís!"* said Fidelma from where she was sprawled out. *"Fine by me."* Fidelma shook her head and laughed. She closed her eyes, it was so peaceful lying here and especially now knowing the wicked Aoife was gone, her family and friends were no longer under threat from her, she hoped the children of Lír would be free some day soon, she went on her first official date with Aaron and he had kissed her. Life felt good. Life felt very good right now. Her thoughts turned suddenly to her Granny, she must have absolutely loved coming here, she probably wished she could live here, she suddenly remembered what Fairy Caoimhe had let slip about her Granny and she made a mental note to question her about it, not today though, today was a day to relax and enjoy everything being right with the world.

Fairy Áines voice interrupted her thoughts "What you thinking about mo chara?" Fidelma half sat up, leaning back on her elbows. "Oh, this and that, you know." Fairy Áine nodded. "Your Granny?" she asked gently. Fidelma smiled to let Fairy Áine know she wasn't sad "My Granny yeah, but also other stuff, just thinking." Fairy Gittan walked over "Fairy Áine?" he said "We should get moving."

They set themselves up again for travel and away they went. The closer they got to their destination the more Fidelma thought she knew where they were headed, she recognised her surroundings. "We're going to the lake aren't we?" she asked Fairy Áine. "There is no fooling you Fidelma is there" laughed Fairy Áine "We thought you would like to see the progress and chat to the children properly, we left them so abruptly the other day." Fidelma nodded. "Yes I'd love to see the progress, and of course chat with the children, I just didn't want to encroach on their privacy with their Father that day, it was such a private moment it felt right to leave." "You are very wise Fidelma" said Fairy Áine.

As they got close to the lake Fidelma could hardly believe her eyes, the bridge looked like it was finished, she could not believe it. "Oh my!" she gasped. Fairy Áine clapped her hands excitedly "Surprise!" she shouted with the other fairies. Tears sprang to Fidelmas eyes, this was actually very emotional. Dilís came to a halt and Fidelma climbed down, she could see the swans gathered at the shore with King Lír and Bodb Derg, some of the Fianna were gathered on the South Mountain. Cailte appeared and made his way towards them, he put his arm around an astounded Fidelma "Well Fidelma, what do you think?" he asked. "I'm literally speechless" she answered "I never imagined you would have the bridge built this quickly." "We have had a lot of men working on it" said Cailte "the Fianna and some of King Lír and Bodb Dergs servants to name but a few." "Thank you" exclaimed Fidelma "I just cannot believe it!" Bodb Derg walked towards them now, Fidelma put her hand out to shake his hand but he threw his arms around her, almost crushing her in a bear hug "Thank you thank you thank you" he said "You have done great things for our family, great things you have done" and he shook her hand vigoursly, Fidelma glanced at Dilís and smiled. Cailte then led Fidelma over to King Lír and the children, King Lír hugged her and the children all nuzzled their heads against her legs. "Are you ready?" Cailte asked her, Fidelma looked at him "Ready" she replied. Cailte took a shell like contraption out of his satchel and blew into it, one of the Fianna men from the South Mountain replied with the same blow of a horn. Fidelma shielded her eyes from the sun and squinted to see the men. It looked like two of them were hammering something into the ground.

All of a sudden what looked like a ball of light flew up from the water and began whizzing around the swans as they huddled together, it was whizzing so fast it looked like a tornado with the swans barely visible within it, then there was a flash and water sprayed up from the lake drenching everyone. The rush of water had taken everyone by surprise so they had all jumped backwards and covered their faces and heads, Fidelma was wiping her wet hair from her face when she caught sight of the children. They were huddled in the same spot, up to their knees in water they began looking at each other and touching each others faces in awe. King Lír and Bodb Derg ran to them and they hugged them and cheered and lifted them up and spun them around. Fidelma turned and hugged Cailte, she then turned to Ardeen who was suddenly by her side and hugged her too. The fairies were all hugging. Fairy Áine flew over to Fidelma. "Congratulations Fidelma" she said with a lump of pride in her throat "This was you, this was all you" she said smiling. "Now this Fidelma is the greatest moment of your life." Fidelma burst into happy emotional tears, the fairies all fluttering at her face, touching her cheeks, wiping tears and clearing her hair out of her wet tears. The next thing the fairies cleared and standing in front of Fidelma was the beautiful Fionnuala. "Fidelma" she said putting out both her hands, Fidelma took her hands "I cannot thank you enough, we are forever in your debt" Fidelma didn't know what to say, she just let go of Fionnualas hands and threw her arms around her. Before she knew it Fidelma was enveloped in a group hug consisting of Fionnuala, Aodh, Fiachra and Conn and then joined by King Lír and Bodb Derg. Fairy Áine was watching from a close distance, tears in her eyes when Cailte walked up to her "An emotional moment for you Fairy Áine" he said simply. Fairy Áine looked at him and wiped her tears away, she lifted her chin as she spoke "I am just incredibely proud of Fidelma."

"Of course" nodded Cailte "of course."

As Fidelma was preparing to leave the lake she climbed aboard Dilís when something caught her eye across the lake. "Fairy Áine!" exclaimed Fidelma "look!" she said pointing towards the North and South mountains. The Fairies all looked to where Fidelma was pointing, before their eyes both mountains were beginning to bloom. The once barren, brown coloured mountains suddenly began sprouting luscious green grass, bright yellow and purple flowers filled the fields. Fidelma felt her heart soar, not only had she saved the children of Lír, but she had reconnected the Man from the North with the Woman from the South.

Chapter 36

They had arrived back at An Crann darach Sean, Cailte had rode back with them. "For the company" he had said. Fidelma was guessing he would be coming in for a cup of tea, she was also guessing he wanted to spend some more time with Fairy Áine. They got down off their horses and once again Dilís told Fidelma he would take himself off to the field, taking Cailtes horse with him. Fairy Áine took Fidelmas hand to bring her in and Fiary Pirkko took Cailtes. As soon as Fidelma got through the door though she was faced with cheering, every single fairy that lived at An Crann darach Sean were standing in front of her waving and cheering. Fidelma looked at Fairy Áine "Surprise" said the fairy "again" and she put her arm around her friend and guided her through to the main room where Fidelma seen the long table was set up with food and drinks. "This looks lovely, thank you" she said to Fairy Áine hugging her tightly. "You are more than welcome" said the fairy. The rest of the fairies all filed in, a few of them picked up their instruments and began playing, in a matter of minutes most of the fairies were up dancing. "You realise you have changed the course of history Fidelma?" Fairy Áine asked. Fidelma looked at the Fairy stunned "Oh my goodness" she exclaimed "are you serious?" Fairy Áine smiled "In this world certainly Fidelma, not in your world though, you understand this legend has already lived out in the New Ireland, sadly nobody was able to save the children then, but you have here." Fidelma beemed, she was so happy right now.

Cailte suddenly came over, grabbed Fidelma and start dancing with her; they were hopping around the room having great fun. "Are you enjoying your party?" Cailte shouted to Fidelma over the music. "Of course I am, who doesn't enjoy their own party?" she laughed in reply. Cailte just smiled at her, he was distracted, he kept glancing over at Fairy Áine as she chatted with her sister. "Why don't you ask her to dance?" Fidelma asked him. Cailte looked at her startled "Who?" he asked. Fidelma shook her head "Fairy Áine of course" she answered. "Ah she is talking to her sister, I don't want to interrupt" he replied. Fidelma smiled mischievously "Leave that to me" she said. And away she went. Fidelma bounded over to the two sisters and grabbed Fairy Fennan by the arm "Come on Fairy Fennan" she shouted at her "Dance with me!" Fairy Fennan shook her head "Ah I'll pass thanks Fidelma." But Fidelma wouldn't take no for an answer "Aw come on" she said "You have to dance with me, it's my party!" The two fairies looked at each other and laughed. "Ok then" giggled Fairy Fennan and she let Fidelma take her out into the throng of dancing fairies. Fidelma danced with Fairy Fennan while keeping a close eye on the progress of Cailte and Fairy Áine. She watched as Cailte approached the fairy, put his hand out to her and speak, she watched as Fairy Áine protested at first but then gave in and took Cailtes hand, she watched as the pair of them laughed while they danced. Fidelma was happy, she was very happy.

Fidelma took a break from the dancing and went over to the table for a drink. She was watching the dancing, tapping her foot to the music as she gulped down a cup of gooseberry juice.

Cailte came over and picked up two cups of juice for himself and Fairy Áine, he clinked his cup to Fidelmas "Thank you" he said. "Not a problem" replied Fidelma "It's good to see her so happy. Oh and thank you for everything, you know, teaching me, guiding me and rounding up the Fianna." "You are more than welcome Fidelma" he said and turned to walk away but Fidelma caught him by the arm. "By the way" she said "you said the Fianna were your uncles army. Who is your uncle?" "Fionn" replied Cailte "Fionn Mc Cumhaill!" and he walked away to rejoin Fairy Áine.

Chapter 37

Fidelma was sitting in her back garden catching the last of the summer rays. In a couple of days she would be back in school. Fairy Áine had told her she would give her a couple of weeks down time before she would come get her again. There were a few things Fidelma wanted to do, she was going to look into Harp lessons for a start. She was also going to see if she could change from French to Home Economics in school, Fidelma couldn't sew a button.

But right now there was something she needed to do, she got up and walked through the kitchen "I'm going out for a bit Mam I'll see you later." And she left the house.

Fidelma knocked on Aaron's front door and he opened it straight away "Hey" he greeted her "I was just about to call for you." Fidelma tilted her head to the side "Can you do me a favour?" she asked. "Of course" replied Aaron. "Grab your jacket; meet me outside my house in 10 minutes." And she ran down the driveway, Aaron laughed and went back inside. Fidelma ran back through her house and out into the garden. At the top of the garden were some Rose bushes, pink, red and pale yellow. Mrs. Doyles pride and joy. Fidelma had lifted her Mothers gardening snippers and began snipping some of the roses off, when she had enough she arranged them into a bunch and walked into the kitchen where Mrs. Doyle was cooking the dinner "Mam" she asked "Have you an elastic band please?" Mrs. Doyle looked at her daughter holding the bouquet of roses "I can do one better; I can give you a nice piece of ribbon if you like?" Fidelma smiled "That'd be perfect Mam thanks."

Mrs. Doyle tied the ribbon around the stems "For someone special love?" she asked her daughter. Fidelma just nodded simply "Yeah Mam, someone special."

Fidelma walked out the door and met Aaron at her gate "Thanks" she said. "No bother" said Aaron "Who are the flowers for?" he asked. Fidelma just replied "Someone special." They walked to the bus stop and sat down on the bench. "Are you gonna tell me where we're going?" Aaron asked her. Fidelma just shook her head. Aaron looked at her then picked up her hand and held it. He knew sometimes Fidelma just needed him to be there. Their bus came; they got on and took a seat.

As they came close to their stop Fidelma let Aaron know "Our stop is next." Aaron looked out the window. "Ok" he said, he looked at the flowers Fidelma was holding and put two and two together, he knew where they were going.

They got off the bus and walked quietly together towards the chapel. Walking through the big black gates Fidelma felt emotional, she had walked through these gates so many times over the years, she used to love going to mass with her Granny. Granny would take her rosary beads from her pocket as soon as they got in and string them through her old bony fingers; she knew every single prayer, every single refrain, every hymn. After mass she would stand beside her Granny as she lit a candle and then she would let Fidelma light one, and tell her to pray for someone who needed prayers. Sometimes if the weather was nice, after mass Granny would take her for a walk through the graveyard, Fidelma never thought it was odd or spooky. Granny would head for the old side of the graveyard where the graves were all more than a hundred years old and they would walk around reading the headstones, Granny would try to string stories together of the people buried there from the inscriptions they read on their headstones, sometimes if a grave was badly overgrown they would clear it.

This evening though, Fidelma was visiting just the one grave. She walked the familiar pathway until she came to her Grannys headstone. It was a tall stone celtic cross, her Granny had ordered and paid for it before she died. Aaron touched the small of Fidlemas back "I'll give you some time" he said quietly and walked away. Fidelma placed the roses on the grave.

"You always loved Mams roses" she said. "Granny" she began "I had no idea the life you were leading, no idea. I always admired you, from the day I was born I admired you, but now" she wiped a tear away "now I admire you even more, if that's possible. I have only been a protector for a few months, but you did it for a lifetime, and you raised your children and looked after your grandchildren. You always had so much time for me, you taught me so much. Thank you." Fidelma let out a little sob. "Thank you so much, for everything, I hope I can make you proud." Fidelma kissed her fingertips and gently touched them to the gravestone, and then she turned away and walked towards Aaron.

Epilogue

Fidelma had been back at school for a couple of weeks and was settling in well. She had managed to change from French to Home Economics without any hassle and she had found someone to give her Harp lessons on Monday evenings. She and Aaron were now officially 'boyfriend and girlfriend' although not a lot had changed; he was still her best friend, except now their parents insisted they keep their door open whatever room they were in.

Fidelma was sitting in her bedroom finishing off her homework when suddenly the treasure chest popped open and out popped Fairy Áine. Fidelma looked at her in surprise happy to see her fairy friend again but then she noticed Fairy Áines expression. "Fidelma!" she exclaimed "I need you to come with me, something's happened."

The End

Printed in Great Britain
by Amazon